Sawyer had to save her.

Straining through the water and the hurricane winds, he reached her Victorian and pounded his fist on the door. “Open this door, Honey, or I’ll kick it in.” His boot leveled a blow against the door.

She opened it, but the wind wrenched it from her grasp. “I don’t need your help.” She jabbed her finger into his slicker. “’Cause unlike you, I don’t walk away and abandon what’s important.”

He ignored her veiled refer[illegible]e to their past. “I’m here to take you to [illegible]

“Being with you, as I[illegible]n’t equal safety.”

He fought to k[illegible]er control. “There’s no [illegible]he water’s rising.”

She tipped h[illegible]ance. “I’m not leaving. And yo[illegible]make me.”

“Watch me.” In two strides he reached her and, seizing her waist, slung her over his shoulder.

“Let go of me!” She pounded his back.

As he slogged through the water, he thought of one thing: it wasn’t the way he’d planned it, but at least she was back in his arms.

Lisa Carter and her family make their home in North Carolina. In addition to her Love Inspired novels, she writes romantic suspense for Abingdon Press. When she isn't writing, Lisa enjoys traveling to romantic locales, teaching writing workshops and researching her next exotic adventure. She has strong opinions on barbecue and ACC basketball. She loves to hear from readers. Connect with Lisa at lisacarterauthor.com.

Books by Lisa Carter

Love Inspired

Coast Guard Courtship
Coast Guard Sweetheart

Coast Guard Sweetheart

Lisa Carter

Recycling programs for this product may not exist in your area.

ISBN-13: 978-0-373-71955-6

Coast Guard Sweetheart

This edition published by arrangement with Love Inspired Books.

www.Harlequin.com

Printed in U.S.A.

Some went down to the sea in ships, doing business on the great waters; they saw the deeds of the Lord, His wondrous works in the deep. For He commanded and raised the stormy wind, which lifted up the waves of the sea.

—*Psalms* 107:23–25

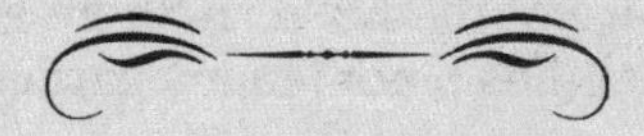

Dedicated to Jean and Billy Davis

Thanks for sharing your heart, home and family with me over these many years. You have been a tremendous blessing in my life.
I love you both.

Mr. Billy—Thank you for helping David dig up the ditch lilies one summer day for us to bring home to North Carolina, allowing me to enjoy a piece of the Eastern Shore every time the lilies bloom in my garden.

Miss Jean—I loved those marsh moccasins you made for us to wear. What a fun time we had that first summer and since—living life, doing ministry together, shopping… Thank you for investing your life in untold numbers of young people and in me.

Acknowledgments

Eastern Shore friends—
Rest assured all fictional hurricane damage was confined to fictional Kiptohanock.

Many thanks to retired United States Coast Guard Captain Jim Umberger for answering my questions about SAR operations. Any errors are my own.

Thanks also to the United States Coast Guard for your dedication and sacrifice. Blessings to you who serve on CG vessels and at CG stations. Thank you for your service.

Chapter One

"What are you doing here, Sawyer Kole?"

Honey Duer's heart stuttered. Irrational gladness surged through her nerve endings until she tamped her feelings down to that secret place where she contained everything concerning the Coast Guard petty officer. Perched on a stool at the Sandpiper Cafe counter, he stiffened at the sound of her voice.

Kiptohanock life ebbed and flowed around them. The hearty scent of eggs and bacon permeated the diner. Weather-beaten watermen packed the green vinyl booths and sopped their buttermilk biscuits in redeye gravy while trading fish stories.

Placing his palms flat against the counter, Sawyer rose and faced her. He let his arms drop to his side.

Much against her will, Honey's gaze locked onto Sawyer's hands—strong, work-roughened and capable. A distant memory flashed of those hands cupping one of Blackie's pups.

The clinking of glasses and murmur of voices in the crowded diner faded into a distant, droning buzz as the image of Sawyer's face that long ago Kiptohanock spring welled in her mind. He'd cradled the black Labrador puppies, the lines fanning out from his eyes as he smiled. At her.

Her stomach knotted. And with her reverie broken, she found his crystal blue gaze fixed on her. In his eyes, she beheld pain, regret, sadness. And a question?

She recalled her crusty waterman father's oft-quoted saying, "Fool me once, shame on you. Fool me twice, shame on me."

Honey quelled the traitorous feelings Sawyer's presence evoked. She'd believed—hoped—after three long years, she'd be immune. But apparently not.

She'd learned the hard way not to trust a Coastie. Especially not this one. So with deliberate effort, she schooled her features and reined in her pulse.

The summer tourist season remained at fever pitch with the upcoming Labor Day weekend and Duck Decoy Festival. And with the Duer family's century-old lodge booked to the rafters, she didn't need this—or him—distracting her.

"Why are you here, Kole?"

Eyelids drooping, he put the stool between them. "Reassigned back to the Shore. Thought the chief would've warned you."

Honey propped her hands on her hips—mainly to give her hands something to do. Anything but allow her hands to shake and betray their utter unreliability. "The chief? Braeden Scott knew you were here?"

Of course as Officer in Charge her brother-in-law knew. Which meant her big sister Amelia knew, too. She growled low in her throat. "How long, Kole? How long have you been skulking around Kiptohanock without me knowing?"

"A week."

Sawyer's eyes, the blue of a winter sky over the blue-green waters of the Delmarva Peninsula, darted toward her again. "I was told you didn't work at the cafe anymore. That you wouldn't be hard to…" His gaze slid away to the diner's plate glass window overlooking the cupola-topped gazebo on the square.

And she extinguished the tiny spark of hope that had surfaced upon spotting his broad uniformed shoulders hunched over a cup of coffee and a plate of Long Johns. As if time had rewound back to that spring when she'd dared to dream, to hope…

She grimaced.

When he left her looking like a fool in front of the fishing hamlet of Kiptohanock, Virginia.

And the startling fact that hope somehow persisted—despite her best efforts to eradicate it—angered Honey. Angered her more than the gall of this here-today, gone-tomorrow Coastie, who had the nerve to show up in her town at her cafe again.

The anger, with three long years to simmer, boiled in her veins. 'Cause Sawyer Kole hadn't come looking for her. He'd come thinking to avoid her.

Eating Long Johns and drinking coffee at her counter as if nothing had changed. Some things never did change. Some men never did, either.

Like how you couldn't trust a Coastie as far as you could throw him.

"Honey, I—" His mouth pulled downward.

The anger percolated in her gut, rising. Someone tugged at her hand.

She glanced down to find her eight-year-old nephew, Max. With whom she'd come searching for a midmorning treat once the inn's guests cleared out after breakfast. Max—whom she'd completely forgotten in her sudden awareness of Sawyer.

"Is that the Coastie who made you cry, Aunt Honey?"

She flinched at the foghorn decibel of Max's voice.

Conversation ground to an abrupt silence.

Sawyer's face constricted and he swallowed. Hard.

"I'm sorry, Honey." Sawyer pivoted on his heel toward the exit.

Her nostrils flared. *That was it?* After all this time, that was all he had to say for himself?

If he thought he was going to walk away from her again, Sawyer Kole had another thought coming. No longer able to contain the molten lava of three years of unanswered questions, her anger erupted and exploded.

"That'd be *Beatrice* Duer to you, Coastie."

She reached across the counter and seized the uneaten Long John on his plate. She hurled the cinnamon donut across the room where it collided with a shower of powdery sugar against the back of Sawyer Kole's hard head.

The dozen or so cafe patrons, including Max, gave a collective gasp.

Sawyer whipped around. The disbelief on his features almost made her laugh.

Almost. 'Cause laughing wasn't something she'd done much since that bittersweet spring.

"Honey..." Her waitress friend, Dixie, lowered a platter of fresh baked Long Johns to the countertop. "Before you go off half-cocked..."

Sawyer just...stared at her. Which only made Honey crazier. She snatched another Long John off Dixie's tray.

This time, he made a gesture with his hand like a stop sign. "Honey..." His mouth tightened.

Honey raised her arm in an arc over her head. "I told you to call me Beatrice. Be-a-trice. Better yet, don't call me anything at all." She drew back.

Sawyer's eyes widened. "You wouldn't..."

Honey lobbed the donut at him.

Zapping him square between the eyes, the Long John

bounced and landed at his regulation black shoes on the cafe's linoleum floor.

"Hah!" She jutted her chin. "I just did."

Max nudged her with his elbow. "Mimi says it's not nice to throw things, Aunt Honey."

"He deserves it." She palpitated another Long John. "This one, too."

And she flung the donut in Sawyer's direction again. But her aim was a trifle off. The Long John only grazed his tropical blue Coastie uniform, leaving a trail of sugar across his chest.

His rugged profile remained stoic. The arctic blue of his eyes smoldered. But otherwise, no reaction.

Maddened, she palmed another pastry, which she let fly in a curveball worthy of the Kiptohanock church league champions. "And another. And—"

It ricocheted off his jaw.

A muscle ticked in his cheek. But he said nothing. Only opened his stance to hip's width and folded his hands behind his back. He lifted his face as if bracing for the next onslaught. Preparing to take whatever she pitched his way.

"Tough guy, huh? I'll show you—"

Max laughed. "This looks like a fun game, Aunt Honey."

Grabbing a Long John for himself, he propelled it across the length of the cafe. It landed with a plop into the cereal bowl of a redheaded girl from his Sunday school class. She screamed as the milk cascaded over the rim and onto her Girl Scout uniform.

Honey made a futile grab for her nephew as he appropriated two fistfuls of fried dough. "Max! Don't—"

But too late.

The little girl yanked a Long John off a fellow scout's plate and chucked it toward Max. But instead of Max, it hit a grungy waterman in the nose.

"Hey!" The boat captain jumped to his feet. His reactionary winged donut walloped the troop leader, Mrs. Francis, upside the head.

Mrs. Francis rose with battle fury in her eyes. "How dare you, you crazy ole—"

"Boys against girls!" Max scrambled atop Sawyer's vacated stool. Using the stool as a shield, with machine-gun rapid fire, he launched the doughy projectiles at the rest of the Girl Scouts.

Who returned fire with targeted accuracy.

Max retreated toward a table of his granddad's contemporaries. Who, when the barrage sailed their way, responded with a volley of catapulted sugar and cinnamon. Ducking behind the padded booths, Mrs. Francis, the Kiptohanock postmistress and the town librarian, directed the Girl Scouts' cannon assault.

"Score!" Max fist-pumped as another donut grenade connected with the little redheaded girl.

Her answering shot left Max with a mouthful of pastry. Spitting and coughing, Max retreated behind the counter.

Donuts a-flying, Sawyer and Honey gaped at the ensuing melee taking place around them. An island of calm in the midst of mayhem.

"Your turn, Aunt Honey."

She dodged too late as the Long John smacked her in the forehead.

Max clenched another pastry in his right hand. "Bull's—"

"Don't do it, Max… Drop it…" Sawyer stepped in front of her and scooped a mangled Long John off the floor. "Don't you dare hit your aunt Honey again, Max."

Max chuckled and took aim. As did Sawyer. Peeping through her fingers, she covered her face with her hands.

The bells jingled as the door whooshed open.

"Executive Petty Officer Kole! What is going on in here? You will cease and desist immediately."

Sawyer groaned at the sight of his boss, Senior Chief Braeden Scott, framed in the doorway of the cafe.

"Max Duer Scott! Honey!"

Honey lowered her hands. Her older sister, Amelia, glared. Max dropped the donut and shuffled his feet.

The surreptitious thud of twenty other donuts hit the floor as the townspeople came to their senses and surveyed the sugary wreckage of Kiptohanock's favorite hangout.

"Storm's a-coming." Seth Duer, her father, crossed his arms across his flannel plaid shirt. "But what in the name of fried oysters is going on in here?"

"What were you thinking, Kole?" Sawyer's superior—and Honey's brother-in-law—stared at him. "We've got a tropical depression barreling up the East Coast and you've started a war in Kiptohanock?"

"I'm sorry, Chief." Sawyer scanned the deserted and wrecked diner. "I accidentally ran into Honey and we sort of...collided."

"Do you think this is a laughing matter, Executive Petty Officer Kole? Do you think this is any way for the second in command at Station Kiptohanock to treat the local populace? Represent the United States Coast Guard? Provide an example to the station crew?"

Sawyer wiped the emerging smile off his face. He went into a rigid salute, feet clamped together. "No. Not at all, Chief Scott."

Braeden glowered. "I should hope not, BMC Kole. Or I might have to rethink requesting your reassignment here on the Delmarva Peninsula."

"Permission to speak freely, Chief?"

Braeden narrowed his eyes. "Ankle deep in powdered sugar, I'd speak carefully if I were you, Kole."

Sawyer cut his eyes around his thirtysomething commander toward the kitchen where the chief's pregnant wife,

Amelia, reamed out a much-subdued Honey. A firm hand clamped on her orphaned nephew and adopted son, Amelia kept Max affixed in place. Fixed like a bug on a pin until his turn for her strawberry blonde wrath.

"This was a bad idea, me being reassigned to the Eastern Shore again, Chief."

Braeden's eyebrow arched. "Oh, really?"

Sawyer nodded. "I thought after what happened three years ago…after our last conversation that night…" He slumped. "That you understood… It was better for everyone, especially Honey, for me to never—"

"What I understand, XPO, is that you acquitted yourself extremely well at your last duty station in California. You are an asset to any boat station, especially this one." Braeden skewered him with a look. "And let me remind you the Coast Guard does not exist for the benefit of the Coastie but the other way around."

Sawyer went into regulation stance again. "Yes, Chief."

Braeden took a deep breath. "However in this case… In the weird—albeit endearing—way of southern families, when Amelia and I got married, the Duers adopted everyone on my side of the marriage, too. Including my father's best friend, Master Chief Davis. And I promise you the Master Chief no more enjoyed watching Honey go from depressed Honey to angry Honey to cynical Honey—"

"I'm guessing we're back at the angry Honey phase." Frowning, Sawyer took a quick, surreptitious look across the cafe.

"Exactly. So one word in the Master Chief's ear and it was no problem getting you reassigned here. Time to work out the unresolved issues chaining the both of you to the past. Nothing worse than might-have-beens. This way—barring a few damaged donuts—better for both of you in the end. Get each other out of your systems."

Braeden's clipped voice gouged at Sawyer's heart. "Or

not, as the case may be. Time to let nature—or donuts—take their course."

"So now we know." Sawyer gulped. "She hates me."

"That what you took from this?" Braeden gestured. "Don't know if I'd agree." Braeden's lips twitched as he surveyed the culinary disaster zone. "I already hear this skirmish is going down in the annals of Kiptohanock lore as The Battle of the Long Johns."

Sawyer smothered a groan. "I'm sorry, Chief. Really sorry. I promise you it won't happen again. I'll perform my duty watches and otherwise keep my distance."

In the corner, the hitherto silent Seth Duer cleared his throat. "That strategy kind of defeats the purpose, don't you think?" The man's bristly mustache twitched.

Sawyer cast his eyes toward the snowy floor.

Honey's dad had never been one of his biggest fans. And rightly so as subsequent events that spring proved. Sawyer was nothing, as his own father routinely declared twenty-odd years ago, if not a self-fulfilling screw-up.

Worthless. Good for nothing. Ruined everyone's life.

Amelia—one hand around the back of Max's scrawny neck and the other squeezing the tender underflesh of Honey's arm—hauled the pair of miscreants toward them.

"Ow, 'Melia." Honey wrested free. "Let go. You're—" Her forward momentum carried her to within an arm's reach of Sawyer.

Honey teetered in her powder-slathered heels. Her eyes flicked toward Sawyer and then to her toes. She clenched and unclenched her hands at her sides.

Sawyer's heart pounded at her proximity.

Beatrice "Honey" Duer was the loveliest woman he'd ever known. As beautiful in her kindness and generosity as her beautiful honey-colored hair and chestnut brown eyes. Seeing her again, despite the circumstances, was both a pleasure and a stabbing ache he'd never quite managed to rid himself of.

He'd never understood until face-to-face now with Honey how one person could inspire within him—all at the same moment—such joy and pain.

This newly embittered, enraged Honey was entirely Sawyer's own fault. A product of his previous misjudgment in allowing the twentysomething Shore girl to get close to him that spring. His father's words—though the man was long dead in a state penitentiary—reverberated in his mind.

Whatever—and whomever—Sawyer touched, he ruined.

Sawyer straightened. "I take full responsibility for what happened here, Chief. My mess. I'll clean it up."

Honey's eyes flickered to his.

Sawyer looked away and focused over her shoulder to the mounted wall map. With his eye, he mentally traced the outline of the Delmarva Peninsula. Delaware. Maryland. Virginia.

His Coast Guard family and his career were the only things he'd ever succeeded at.

Sawyer kept his posture tall and his feet pointed toward Braeden. "I also want to compensate the Sandpiper owner for lost revenue and supplies, Chief."

Honey bristled.

Sawyer sneaked a glance her way before resuming his perusal of the framed map.

The Atlantic Ocean. The Chesapeake Bay. Highway 13. Chincoteague. Onley. Nassawadox. Willis Wharf. Kiptohanock nestling on the Great Machipongo Inlet.

His Coast Guard family and career were also the only things in his life he'd not ruined or self-sabotaged. Until now.

Sawyer steeled himself. "I understand you'll have to

file an official reprimand in my service record. And if I'm demoted and transferred—"

Honey's breath hitched. "Wait. This wasn't his fault." She caught hold of Braeden's sleeve. "I started it. Not him. I'm to blame. He shouldn't be punished for defending himself."

Sawyer angled. "You don't have to..."

Her face clouded. "Actually, he was defending me. I'll reimburse Dixie and the owner for lost wages. I'll clean—"

"You're *all* going to clean up this mess, baby girl." The jean-clad Seth unwound from where he leaned against a booth. "You, Guardsman Kole here and—" He harpooned Max with his hand and reeled him closer. "And my grandson, Max, too."

Mutiny written across his features, Max squirmed. "But I'm s'posed to go with Mimi and Dad for Mimi's doctor visit."

The very pregnant Amelia sidled next to her husband, Braeden. "Granddad's right, Max. Every action has consequences. Time for you to own yours."

"But—but..."

"No buts." Braeden bent to Max's level. "A good Coastie learns to accept responsibility for his actions."

He speared Sawyer with a look. "You've got major damage control to take care of here, Kole. Not to mention prepare for a late season storm threatening landfall anywhere between Delaware and Charleston, South Carolina, over the next few days."

Sawyer nodded. "Affirmative, Chief. The cafe will be shipshape by the time you and the missus return this afternoon."

"I'm counting on it." Braeden straightened to his full height. "I know I can also count on you and Honey to supervise my boy, Max, until I return. Giving him an example of what integrity looks like."

Seth moved toward the door. "I've got a short charter this morning, but I expect a full report from you, XPO Kole, when I return midday. Me and you are going to have a chat. Long overdue, in fact. You roger that?"

"Daddy… This has nothing to do with you." Honey frowned. "Why are you always trying to ruin my life?"

Sawyer went ramrod stiff at the echo of his own thoughts. "Roger, Mr. Duer. I'll be waiting for you on the harbor dock."

Honey's father exchanged glances with Braeden and Amelia. "I'm not trying to ruin your life, baby girl. Can't nobody do that to you but you."

Flushing, Honey drew a circle in the confectioner's sugar with the toe of her shoe.

Heading out, Seth settled his ball cap firmly about his graying head and adjusted the brim. "Something you ought to ponder as you're cleaning up this mess the two of you made."

Chapter Two

After several hours of cleanup, Honey stole a look at Sawyer's shuttered face as she handed him another rinsed plate to towel dry.

Standing on the other side of the stainless steel commercial sink, he refused to meet her gaze. In the adjacent dining area, Max—his usual no-holds barred bravado gone—mopped up the remains of their shared folly.

For a moment, she allowed herself the pleasure of lingering on Sawyer's craggy Nordic features. His features once as familiar to Honey as her own.

The straw-colored, stick-straight hair cut in a Coastie buzz. Same brawny muscular build, which befitted the former rodeo rider and boat-driving coxswain.

His sharp bone structure and hooded brow missed handsome by a smidgeon. But somehow it suited him better. And to Honey's way of thinking always made him more fascinating. At least to her.

Yet she noted new lines bracketing his mouth since the last time she'd seen him. A hairline scar on his chin. A somberness out of place on the puddle pirate, full-throttle Coastie she'd previously known.

And loved beyond all reasoning. Until he'd broken off

their relationship one night on a deserted moonlit beach outside Ocean City for no explicable reason.

Three summers of unanswered questions as to why Sawyer Kole so abruptly ended their burgeoning romance fairly burned a hole in her tongue. And as for her brother-in-law, newly appointed Officer in Charge of USCG Small Boat Station Kiptohanock? Make that her former favorite brother-in-law, Braeden Scott.

Honey had a few choice words for mother hen big sister Amelia, too. After their mother's early death, Amelia had semiraised Honey. But how dare Amelia keep Sawyer's transfer a secret and allow Honey to be blindsided by him? Her cheeks reddened at the memory of how once before his rejection exposed her to total public humiliation in the eyes of the close-knit fishing community.

Small towns. Small minds. Big mouths.

And after today's incident... Okay...that was on Honey's head.

But enough with the suffocating silence. "Look, Kole..."

Her deliberate use of his surname accomplished her intended effect. His lips flattened into a tight line. And something else—hurt—flickered across his eyes before his customary aloofness returned.

Yet somehow her small victory felt hollow. Much less satisfying than she'd imagined in the thirty-nine months, five days and ten hours since he'd broken her heart.

But who was counting, right?

Distracted by the nearness of him, Honey fought to convey a nonchalance she didn't feel. Not with Sawyer a mere elbow's length away. Not when every traitorous, torturous nerve ending quivered with longing every time he breathed.

She found it hard to breathe with Sawyer Kole this close. So she settled for sighing to release her pent-up store of oxygen.

"For whatever reason, we've been the victims of a Duer/ Scott conspiracy. I'm assuming you returned to Station Kiptohanock under duress."

Sawyer concentrated on drying the plate. "A Coastie goes where a Coastie is assigned."

"And where have you been assign—never mind." Honey gave her head a tiny shake. "Not that I care what you've been doing all this time. I've been plenty busy reopening the Duer Fishermen's Lodge." She tucked a wavy curl behind her ear.

Sawyer's eyes followed the movement of her hand. "I heard through the village grapevine about the inn. How your hard work is paying off. Your dreams coming true."

"This season is critical for turning a profit. Make it or break it. After finally branding the lodge as a premier Tidewater wedding venue, I don't need any more grief from you or those with mistaken notions about my own good."

His face shadowed. He folded the dishtowel into meticulous thirds on the drain board. "I expect this peninsula—if not this village—is big enough for the two of us, Hon—" He grimaced. "I mean—Beatrice. I promise I'll do my best to stay out of your way."

"I'd like to tell you what I think of your promises, cowboy. But I won't." She shoved off from the sink. "What you can do is explain to me why you cut anchor and sailed out of my life three years ago. I think you owe me that at least."

Hunching, he crossed his arms over his broad chest, momentarily distracting Honey.

Sawyer tucked his thumbs under his biceps and out of sight. "I'm sorry for hurting you. But better I hurt you before you got in over your head."

Her eyebrows rose. "Before *I* got in over my head, Coastie? Speak for yourself."

Sawyer glanced away.

Her stomach churned. Why wouldn't he look at her?

Was she so repellant to him that he still couldn't bear facing her? If only she knew what she'd said or done…

Or had he walked away for greener pastures? She'd been an idiot to believe he was any different from the skirt-chasing Coastie who'd abandoned her dead oldest sister, Lindi, and baby Max.

"Let me get this through my obviously thickheaded Eastern Shore dumb blonde skull, Kole."

She grabbed hold of his chin between her thumb and forefinger, and jerked his gaze to hers. Electric fire sparked between her fingertips and his skin. She dropped her hand.

He edged out of her reach. "I had my reasons."

She rubbed her tingling fingers against the side of her skirt and gathered the remnants of her self-respect. "So you're sorry you hurt me, but not sorry you left me? And you still don't have the decency to tell me why."

A vein beat a furious tempo in his cheek. Her heart pounded at the bleak expression on his face. Her eyes stung. She was so done with crying over this cowboy.

Confusion and misery rose in equal measure, twisting her insides. "I wish," Honey spat, "you'd stayed in that black Oklahoma hole that you crawled out of."

Sawyer flinched as if she'd struck him. He closed his eyes for a second as if absorbing the blow. And when he opened his eyes?

Her heart wrenched, leaving her feeling like she'd just kicked a dog when it was down.

"I think…" That slow, cowboy drawl of his cracked a trifle. He cleared his throat and surveyed the Sandpiper kitchen. Once more refusing to meet her gaze.

Or answer her questions.

"I think between us, we've done about as much as we can to repair the damage." He took a ragged breath. "But I wish…"

She strained forward, but Sawyer choked off the rest and hurried toward the dining room.

What? What did Sawyer wish?

He yanked open the glass-fronted door, setting the bells into a furious jingle.

She stared until the door whooshed shut behind him. She monitored his quick, determined stride across the parking lot separating the CG station from the cafe. With a sinking heart, she watched him disappear toward the end of the Kiptohanock town pier.

"You're mean, Aunt Honey."

Max hung over the cutout window, elbows planted in place. She wondered how long he'd perched there. How much he'd overheard.

"I don't like you today." His lower lip trembled. "And I don't want to stay with you and Granddad this summer while that stupid baby's born." Max frowned. "Inside I feel as mean as you treated Sawyer."

Remorse fretted at her conscience. What was wrong with her? She used to never be this way. That is, not until Sawyer had cut her heart to the quick.

"Is that why Mimi left me here? 'Cause I'm so mean?"

"No, Max." She reached for him. "You're not mean. Amelia had to go to her doctor appointment. Like last month. She told you why you couldn't come today."

Max slung his legs over to the kitchen side. "I want her to come home. I want things to be the way they used to be before…" He shook his head. "But once the other boy comes nothing will ever be the same."

She gathered him close. "Mimi and Braeden love you. That is something that will never change."

Max leaned his forehead against hers. "Do you think she wanted this baby 'cause I got too big to hold? I tried not to grow. Honestly." He captured her face.

She ignored the gritty feel of his palms on her skin

and focused on his blueberry eyes where moisture welled. "Oh, Max."

Max had been born mere hours before his dying mother, Lindi, the oldest Duer daughter, bequeathed her infant son into the trustworthy hands of Amelia. And when Max turned two? Honey shuddered to recall those horrible years after Max was diagnosed with childhood leukemia. How she, Dad and most especially Amelia—Max's beloved Mimi—suffered with the little boy through every treatment until he reached remission.

The frail, sickly boy Braeden Scott first met had been replaced by this healthy, suntanned, mischievous bundle of energy. This same redheaded boy had been instrumental in Amelia finding her own happily-ever-after with the handsome Coastie Scott.

"Nothing will change when this baby's born, Max. Only then, you'll have someone else to play with and love, too."

"It won't be the same..." His voice dropped.

She kissed his forehead. "It'll be better, Max. Better than before, I promise." His skin tasted of cinnamon sugar, a legacy from the Long John war.

"Like Sawyer promised?" Max peered at her. "I like Sawyer. Don't you remember when he—"

"When he showed his true character." Honey remembered that glorious spring far too well. "Sawyer Kole doesn't keep his promises. Me you can trust, Max. Him, I can't afford to."

Sawyer grabbed the mooring line Seth Duer threw to him. He secured the rope around the cleat on the Kiptohanock wharf. Motorboats and other small fishing vessels also docked alongside the pier. The briny aroma of sea salt perfumed the air.

He took a deep, steadying breath.

Because this conversation promised to be about as fun

as sitting on a desert cactus. Unpleasant, but a necessary part of Sawyer's self-prescribed penance. He'd hurt this man's daughter. Sawyer prepared himself to be slugged in the jaw and dropped in the Machipongo drink. All of which he deserved.

And more.

"Mr. Duer, sir."

His hand hard with calluses, Seth passed him one of the now empty bait buckets. Sweat broke out on Sawyer's forehead at the older man's unnerving silence. He stepped back as Honey's father hoisted the other bucket onto the pier. And with a light-footedness that denied his fifty-odd years, the rugged Shoreman bridged the gap between the *Now I Sea* and the dock.

The wiry waterman brushed his hand over the top of the mounted iron bell on the end of the pier. A bell, Sawyer remembered, used only for the annual blessing of the fleet at the start of the fishing season in spring. And to summon the villagers in times of maritime disaster.

"I'm assuming the Sandpiper has been restored to proper working order."

Sawyer nodded. "Yes, sir."

"You starting your two days on or two days off, son?" Seth squinted at him, his eyes a variation of the blue-green teal many of the Shore residents sported. "May I call you, son?"

Sawyer swallowed past the large boulder lodged in his throat. If only his own father had been a tenth of the man Seth Duer was.

How often that spring he spent with Honey he'd envied her strong, loving family. Envied the faith that bound the community together. Wished he had somewhere and someone to call home.

A seagull's cry broke the silence. Sawyer realized that

Seth Duer still awaited his response, the old waterman's head cocked at an angle.

"I'd—I'd be honored, sir. It's my two days off."

Honey's father studied him. Sawyer remained still under his gristly-browed scrutiny, ready to take whatever blow Seth dealt him. Something Sawyer had learned from *his* no-good drunken excuse for a father.

The older man blew a breath out between his lips. "Braeden's right," he declared in that gravelly smoker voice of his. "You're not the same brash boy who left here three years ago."

Oh, how Sawyer prayed he wasn't.

Sawyer trained his eyes on the inlet that meandered past the barrier islands until emptying into the Atlantic. A cormorant dive-bombed for fish in the marina. With the wind picking up, seagulls wheeled aloft in graceful figure eights.

"I know what you did for my daughter."

His gaze swung to Honey's father. "*For* your daughter, sir? Don't you mean *to* your daughter?"

"The sacrifice you made." The waterman scrubbed his hand over his stubbly jawline. "Reckon you believed you were doing her a favor. Saving her future heartache. Didn't turn out that way, though. That's why I put a word into Braeden's ear. Why I asked, if possible, you receive a temporary posting to settle things once and for all."

"You were the one?" Sawyer jammed his hands in his pockets. "I figured you'd be the one meeting me at the Bridge with a shotgun."

The old man grinned. "Don't think that idea didn't cross my mind three years ago."

Sawyer inserted his finger between his neck and his collar. And tugged. Despite the bracing sea breeze keeping the marina flags aflutter, the air had grown a bit too close for comfort.

"You've got your current chief, Braeden Scott, to thank for saving your life once upon a spring night."

"Chief's been a good friend. Better than I deserved. The brother I always wished I had."

Tenacious about staying in touch the past three years wherever Sawyer found himself assigned. Three long years when all he could do was lick his wounds and work hard to make his CG mentor proud.

"Braeden also told me about your past, son."

Sawyer reddened. "He shouldn't have done that, sir. I—I—" He dropped his eyes to the gray-weathered planks unable to face Seth Duer.

The old man heaved a sigh. "I understand better than you could ever know."

He darted a glance at the waterman's face as a faraway look crossed Seth Duer's stern countenance. "I'm not the kind of man Honey deserved. Wouldn't have been a welcome addition to the Duer clan like Braeden."

Seth gave him a faint smile. "I wouldn't be too sure about that or Honey if I were you."

He opened his palms. "I promise you, Mr. Duer, I'll stay far away from Honey till my permanent reassignment comes through. Braeden—I mean Chief Scott—promised if I'd give it through Labor Day, he'd arrange a transfer."

"Well, here's the thing, son." Seth removed his Nandua Warriors ball cap and resettled it upon his head. "Honey ain't that sweetly naive girly-girl you remember. In fact, she's become a highly driven, successful entrepreneur with more sharp edges than a barracuda."

Sawyer clamped his lips together.

"The Martha Stewart wannabe has become the Hostess with the Mostest on our fair Eastern Shore." Seth ground his teeth. "She's about to drive us crazy with her doilies and tea cakes and dressed-to-impress agenda. She's about driven me out of house and home."

Seth drew his brows together in a frown. "Not to mention every man within a Shore-wide radius, including the ever-faithful Charlie Pruitt—"

Bracing himself, Sawyer squared his jaw.

"—Driven us stark raving insane with her prickly, self-imposed perfectionism."

Something tightened in Sawyer's chest.

"After pondering long and hard on the situation," Honey's father took a cleansing breath. "We—the Duer clan—need your help."

"Need my help? How?"

"The girl," Seth rolled his tongue over his teeth. "I'm speaking plainly to you now, son. The girl needs a course direction. She needs to be reeled in and brought to her senses before it's too late. Before she drives away everyone who tries to love her. The hurt's festering in her soul. She won't let it heal. No time for life. No time for love. No house, no career can fill the emptiness inside that girl."

Guilt for his part in Honey's pain ate Sawyer alive.

"There's nothing I'd like more than to make things right for her." Sawyer gave a hopeless shrug. "But she hates me, Mr. Duer. Flat out can't stand the sight of me, not that I blame her."

Honey's dad eyed him. "Thought you Coastie boys were perceptive." Seth stroked his bristly mustache with his index finger. "Hatred, I assure you, son, is not what that girl of mine feels for you. Quite the opposite, I imagine."

Sawyer shuffled his feet. "I'll apologize to her again—in a less dangerous setting than the Sandpiper—"

Old Man Duer grinned, rearranging the wrinkles on his face.

"—So she and—" This part made Sawyer want to puke right into the tidal marsh. "So Honey and that—that Charlie Pruitt can find their happily-ever-after."

"Pruitt, huh?" Seth grunted. "Love is so wasted on the

young." His mouth contorted. "The both of you make me tired. After the work that went into getting 'Melia and Braeden together, I hoped I was done with the hard cases. I'm too old for this romantic nonsense."

The waterman squelched in his Wellingtons a few feet toward the parking zone until turning. "You got till Labor Day to clean up this mess with Honey and bring back my sweet girl, Petty Officer Kole. You owe me. You owe Honey that much. You read me?"

Sawyer's Adam's apple bobbed. "Loud and clear, sir. Loud and clear."

Chapter Three

"What were you thinking, Honey?" her sister scolded. "Though that's the problem, I expect. One look at Sawyer Kole and you stopped thinking. Just reacted."

Honey fluffed the pillow behind Amelia's head. "Yeah. I saw red."

Amelia smirked. "Red like a Valentine heart."

"Kole should be so lucky."

Honey made an effort to wrest her mind from the recent unpleasantness. "Anyway, I'm thrilled you, Max and Braeden are Shoreside. It may not be Hawaii, but it's good to finally have you home."

Amelia patted a spot beside her on the bed. "The past two years have been incredible with Braeden assigned to the Pacific fleet." She winked. "Great place for a honeymoon, too."

Honey eased next to her sister. "Don't go getting any ideas. Sawyer and I are so not happening. And don't think the doctor putting you on bed rest this last month of your pregnancy is going to save you from the Wrath of Honey after what you, Braeden and Dad pulled. Y'all got him reassigned. Thanks a lot. Exactly what I didn't need."

"Just trying to achieve closure for you, baby sis. With Sawyer or not, time for you to move on toward everything

God has for your future." Amelia arched an eyebrow. "I remember you once laid that line on me when I dithered over whether to trust Braeden."

Honey stood abruptly, moving to the window. A gentle sea breeze rustled the shade trees that studded the front lawn of the Duer Lodge. "I also told you Braeden's the picture in the dictionary beside *gentleman* and *trustworthy*."

She fingered the lacy curtain and peered down the length of the white picket fence lining the edge of the tidal creek property. "Trust *me* when I tell you, Sawyer Kole is neither of those qualities."

Honey twisted the pearl on her earlobe. Mom's pearl earrings. That and this house were her last links to the mother she'd lost when only a little older than Max.

"I know he hurt you, Honey. I'd never make light of the pain you've suffered, but perhaps he had his reasons, which seemed right to him at the time."

Honey whirled. "Reasons? That's what Sawyer said." She clenched her fist. "What reason could there possibly be for torpedoing the future I was stupid enough to...?" She paced Amelia's childhood bedroom. "That arrogant, no-good cowboy—"

Amelia ignored her and retrieved the sketchpad and pencil she'd left on the nightstand. "Before you go all judgmental, you might want to consider Sawyer might have wounds of his own you know nothing about."

Honey halted. "You know something, don't you?"

Chewing the inside of her cheek, Amelia buried her head in her sketches.

"You know what made him break off the relationship... You've got to tell me." Honey flopped on the bed. "Amelia, look at me." She grabbed for Amelia's arm.

The pencil swerved in Amelia's hand.

"Honey..." Amelia groaned. "I'm on a deadline. My

publisher expects these Hawaiian rainforest birds finished, bed rest and romantic crisis or not."

Amelia ripped off the ruined drawing. "And no, I'm not going to tell you what I know. It's Sawyer's story to tell. If you'd give him a chance—"

"Give him another go at my heart? I think not. I'd sooner be oyster roasted." Honey flung out her hands. "Clam baked. Crab deviled."

"Stop with the food analogies. You're making me hungry." Amelia skimmed her fingertips over her basketball-size belly. "Baby, too. And I'm already the size of a beached whale."

Honey's lips quirked. "An attractive beached whale, though."

"Love you, too, sister." But Amelia smiled.

Honey folded her arms over her pink It's a Shore Thang T-shirt. "Speaking of the baby, you and Braeden need to talk to Max. He's not dealing so well with 'Baby Makes Four.'"

She relayed her conversation with Max at the Sandpiper.

Amelia's gaze roamed to her wedding photo on the bureau. "I thought we dealt with his insecurity before we left Hawaii. He loved it there, but he was so happy to come home to his old room and see you and Dad."

Honey picked up the picture frame. "Glad to see his dog, Blackie, you mean. Dad and I missed you, too." She studied the photo of Amelia's gorgeous barrier island wedding. "Such a happy day. Three years ago this Labor Day."

"Now a different kind of labor day awaits."

Amelia mock-groaned and reached for the pillow behind her back.

Honey laughed and skipped out of range. "And school starts as usual the day after, but I've promised Max we'll go clamming in between visitors this weekend. Dad will keep him busy as first mate on the fishing charters, too."

"May not be many charters." Amelia cut her eyes toward the window. "Sky's still blue, but Dad says his bones tell him a storm's coming."

Honey massaged her forehead. "Please, no. Not before the Labor Day weekend. It's summer's last hurrah and I can't afford any cancellations."

She shifted from one fuchsia polka dot flip-flop to the other. "Maybe the storm will weaken once it leaves the Caribbean. Better yet, give the Shore a wide berth and blow itself far, far out to sea."

Amelia shrugged. "If an Eastern Shoreman like Dad thinks it's coming..."

"It's coming," Honey moaned.

"Which means Braeden and the station crew will be busy preparing for the worst case scenario. You know their motto, Always Ready."

"Coasties." Honey set the photo with a firm thud onto the pine bureau. "You've gone soft with marriage and a new baby, 'Melia."

Amelia sent a pointed look in Honey's direction. "And you've gone cynical and bitter."

Honey tossed her hair over her shoulder. "Courtesy of a Coastie and the pain of unrequited love."

"You sure it's unrequited?"

Honey batted her eyes. "Pretty sure since *he's* the one who left *me* crying on the beach."

"What happened to the Duer sister who dreamed of reopening the Duer Lodge? Who single-handedly restored this old house? Who juggles finicky tourists, placates jittery brides and also manages to keep dear ole Dad on the straight and narrow with his heart medication?"

Honey spun on her heel. "I'll tell you what happened to her. Sawyer Kole happened to her. Plus a stagnant economy. Tourism in the tank. The yet unpaid debt on the remodel. I'm not bitter. I'm a realist."

"I liked the old Honey better."

Honey fought to keep her lips from trembling. Actually, so did she. But she'd never admit that to Amelia or anyone else. She'd poured all her passion and all her drive into making the inn an Eastern Shore vacation and wedding destination.

Talk about black holes? She felt as if she'd fallen into one ever since Sawyer walked out of her life. And truth be told, she didn't know how to free herself from the whirling maelstrom of doubt and sadness in which she found herself trapped.

"So you don't believe in second chances, Honey? In forgiveness?"

"Why should I? Not like Lindi ever got a second chance before getting creamed by the drunk driver. Or Mom before the cancer killed her."

Amelia sucked in a breath. "Honey… I never knew you felt that way."

"Yeah, that was the old Honey. Smile though your heart is breaking. But you know my new motto, There's Nothing Life Throws at You That Sweet Tea And the Duer Lodge Can't Cure."

"Maybe you should give forgiveness a try."

"Maybe God should have given Mom and Lindi another chance."

Amelia's mouth quivered. "That's what this is about, isn't it? You're mad at God."

"Oh, I'm not just mad at God. I'm mad at myself. I'm mad for trusting that cowboy Coastie in the first place. Believing we could ever have a life together."

She jutted her chin. "Well, I've made a life. A life for myself right here on the Shore. A life without Sawyer Kole. I've created an oasis of calm and elegance and class where no one can ever hurt me again."

Amelia caught hold of her hand. "Sounds like a lonely

life. I'm sorry Braeden got reassigned so soon after we were married. I'm sorry I wasn't here for you."

"Don't ever be sorry for your happily-ever-after, big sis." She gently extricated herself from Amelia's grasp. "You deserve every happiness in the world."

"So do you, baby sis."

Honey leaned and gave her sister a quick kiss on the cheek. "I'm not that baby you and Dad have to watch out for anymore, 'Melia. I'm grown up now, and I can take care of myself. This inn proves it."

"You don't have to prove anything to me or Dad, Honey."

"Prove it to myself then. And this town. Especially after the way I acted the fool despite your warnings about here today, gone tomorrow Coasties. You were kind to never say 'I told you so.' Some of the older village ladies weren't so kind, believe me."

"Is that why you haven't been to church in a year? You know how those town ladies talk. Too much time on their hands. Besides, we grew up worshipping there. It's always been such a safe haven, a sanctuary of peace."

"A safe haven for you maybe. Not for me." Honey pushed back her shoulders. "This house is my sanctuary."

"Oh, Honey…"

"It's true. Only safe haven I need. And anyway, Sunday morning breakfasts are a big deal. Part of the advertised package. A long, leisurely time for guests to relax before checking out and returning to their stressful off-Shore lives."

Amelia frowned. "I'm not going to stop praying for you. And for your happily-ever-after, too."

"Pray away. Though I'd appreciate it more if you and God could get this storm to take a detour away from the Eastern Shore and my bottom line. Not everybody is lucky enough to have a Max and Braeden in their life."

"Not lucky, Honey. Blessed."

"Whatever. Speaking of Max, time for me to pick him up at Mr. Billy's house. He was excited about feeding the baby goats, but I promised Max as soon as I got you settled we'd spend the rest of the afternoon clamming in the tidal marsh."

After leaving her sister, Honey did a quick check of the guest bedrooms in the Victorian inn. Fresh towels hung from the en suite bathrooms she'd installed at tremendous cost. She'd already changed the sumptuous bed linens before leaving for the Sandpiper this morning.

She'd have a full house this weekend if the storm didn't scare the tourists away. And the big wedding scheduled on the lawn for Sunday should be fine. Although the bride from off-Shore with her last-minute demands might make Honey lose her carefully wrought reputation for no-hitch weddings, not to mention her mind. But with the deep-pocketed father of the bride renting out the entire property—inn, cabin and dock—for the day, Honey could afford to give his diva daughter some leeway.

Her current guests were no doubt busy kayaking through the Inner Passage off Kiptohanock. Birding, boating and doing a hundred other Eastern Shore activities she and the Accomack County Tourist Board had worked so hard to highlight. So far, so good. This season had been a tremendous success and blessing—she grimaced.

Amelia, get out of my head.

With registration complete for the day and her guests otherwise occupied till breakfast the next morning, the rest of the day belonged to Honey. She had yeast rolls rising in the commercial-grade kitchen and a load of laundry going in the front-loading washer on the back screened porch. Off limits to non-Duers.

She trailed her hand down the graceful, curving banister as she did a look-see of the downstairs common area. Guests found her dad's piecrust table checkerboard folksy. The sea glass and driftwood decor she'd collected from the barrier island charming and beachy. The knotted pine interior rustic and homey.

Homey Honey. That was her.

She straightened an errant sofa cushion, which had gone *catabiased*—to use one of Dad's favorite Eastern Shore expressions. And as usual, whenever in the remodeled family room, her gaze drifted to the one thing she refused to change. The Duer family portrait taken on the lawn overlooking the inlet. Taken when everything had been safe in her childhood world.

Before Caroline went off to college and never returned. Before Mom succumbed to cancer. Before Dad lost himself to a decade of grief. Before her oldest sister, Lindi—like Honey—unwisely loved a Coastie and in the process paid for it with her life.

Other than Honey's nonexistent love life, things were better now. With Amelia happily married, Max healthy and whole, and her dad once more in business with his oldest love, the sea, Honey had the time to make her fondest dream a reality—bringing the Duer Lodge back to life. Home to seven generations of Duers, Virginia watermen one and all.

During the last century, Northern steel magnates roughed it at the Duer's fisherman lodge while her ancestors oystered and served as hunting guides in the winter. Crabbed and ran charters in the summer. The lodge's heyday—and the steamers from Wachapreague to New York City—had long ago passed into history. But with Honey's hand on the proverbial rudder?

What had once been lost would finally be regained.

She bit her lip.

If only everything else in her life could be so easily restored.

* * *

Sawyer drove around the Kiptohanock village square, occupied by the cupola-topped gazebo.

Not much had changed in the seaside hamlet. The post office and bait shop. The white-steepled clapboard church. The CG station. Boat repair business. Victorian homes meandered off side lanes.

But he'd not understood until he left this place behind three years ago how much the village and its hardy fishing folk had seeped into his heart.

Especially Honey.

By his own choice, he'd believed himself cut off from her forever. And he'd worked hard—on and off duty—to forget her. To no avail.

The emptiness remained no matter what he did. California girls had not proven—like Honey's favorite song declared—to be the best in the world for him. He'd stopped hanging out with the guys when off watch. Because nothing stopped the ache in his chest when he thought of the doe-eyed girl he'd left behind on the Eastern Shore of Virginia.

Nothing and no one—until that last tragic search and rescue off the coast of San Diego. At the end of his strength—mental, physical and spiritual—he'd reached in a last desperate attempt for the God the Duers served. And in the reaching—he'd been found.

And in turn found peace. Sufficient to wash away the sadness and the fears. More than enough for any situation he faced.

It had been the picture of the white-steepled church hugging the shoreline of coastal Kiptohanock that came to his mind amidst the uncertainty and fear of that mission gone wrong. The steeple—rising like a beacon of hope above the tree line as the boats came into harbor—which he remembered when pitted against the elements in a life and death struggle. The image kept him tethered to life in those horrible hours in the Pacific when he struggled to survive.

The steeple—a lifeline of hope and mercy. A lifeline that led afterward to a relationship with the Creator of the vast and deep.

A relationship Sawyer looked forward to nurturing. There was so much this former foster kid needed to learn. Unlike the Duers, his backside had never darkened a church pew until recently.

He was eager before he shipped out again to find out more about this God Braeden and the Duers served at the small, country church in Kiptohanock. Braeden had encouraged him to meet with Reverend Parks. But in the secret places of his heart, Sawyer worried like a dog with a bone whether God could ever really love someone like him.

Sawyer shook his head to clear the troublesome thoughts as he followed Seaside Road, which paralleled the main Eastern Shore artery of Highway 13 on one side and the archipelago of shoals, spits and islands that dotted the ocean side. He turned into the long dapple-shaded Duer drive.

Thrusting open the door of his truck, he took a quick breath for courage. His sneakers crunched across the oyster-shelled path leading to the wraparound porch. Where he found the very pregnant Amelia ensconced on a white wicker chaise lounge chair, sipping a tall cool glass of sweet tea.

His mouth watered. Another thing this Oklahoma boy missed about the Eastern Shore and the South. That and Amelia Scott's sister.

Amelia deposited her glass with a plunk onto the small table at her elbow.

His eyes narrowed.

Their last encounter—with Amelia declaring his utter unfitness to be a part of her baby sister's life—had not gone well. And there was the harpoon incident the first time she met her future husband whom she mistook for an intruder. A case of mistaken identity, which three happily married years later, Braeden still liked to joke about.

Amelia gestured toward the pitcher. "Want some tea?"

Sawyer moistened his lower lip with his tongue, but he shook his head. "No, ma'am. Thank you, though."

He stayed on the bottom step, ready to flee should Amelia decide to chuck the contents at him. Couldn't be too careful with these Duer girls.

She scrunched her face, wrinkling the freckles sprinkling the bridge of her nose. "You make me feel so old when you call me ma'am. But I can't fault your manners. Someone taught you well."

His gaze swept across the black urns filled with fire-engine red geraniums positioned on either side of each planked step. That would've been the last foster mom who'd encouraged him to give rodeo a try.

"What did you come here for, Sawyer?"

His eyes darted upward. "I came for Honey."

She laughed.

He flushed. "I—I mean I came to talk to her. To apologize before I head out in a few days."

Amelia skewered him with a look.

He shuffled his feet.

"I think you said exactly what you meant the first time." She reached for her glass. "And don't be in such a rush to leave us again."

He stuffed his hands into the pockets of his cargo shorts. "Is she in the house? Could I talk to her? Will she talk to me?"

"It's low tide." Amelia brought the tea glass to her lips. "She and Max went clamming."

His heart sank. "Oh."

"But no reason you can't take the extra kayak and head

out into the marsh to find them. With Max along, she won't have gone far."

He raised his eyebrow into a question mark. "With Max along, is there any point in me trying to talk to her?"

Amelia's lips curved into a smile. "With Max along, it may save you from getting clam raked. She'll keep it civil in front of him." Amelia glanced toward the sky. "I hope."

She motioned behind the house to where the lawn sloped to the Duer dock. "Go on. Time's a-wasting. Three years a-wasting, if you get my drift."

"I've never been clamming. I don't know where to look for them."

"Keep paddling until you find the dirtiest, muckiest patch of marsh mud and there they'll be."

He nodded. "Thank you, Mrs. Scott. I wanted to tell you how sorry I am for upsetting you that spring, too." He forced himself to look into Amelia's blue-green eyes.

The compassion—and forgiveness—he beheld there made his chest tighten.

"You also saved my life that spring, Sawyer. Pulled me out of the Kiptohanock harbor while Braeden saved Max from his own impulsiveness. And it's Amelia. Or 'Melia to friends like you."

His eyes widened. "After what happened… I'm surprised you'd want me as a friend. Or allow me to get within a nautical mile of Honey."

Amelia cocked her head. "I'm glad you're back. A new, better man, Braeden tells me. And I know Honey will be glad you're back, too. Once she gets over being furious with you."

He planted his feet even with his hips. "Don't know I'll be here long enough for that to happen. She's plenty mad."

"She's also plenty in love with you, XPO Kole."

He fought the moisture in his eyes. "I—I can't wish for

that, 'Melia. Can't allow myself to hope. I never did deserve Honey. Still don't."

"It's not about being good enough, Sawyer."

He hunched his shoulders.

Amelia sighed. "I hope you'll join us at church this Sunday before you leave. I wish Honey would, too. But she won't. Hasn't come in a long time."

Something else to lay at his revolving door of never-ending guilt.

God help him, Sawyer had so much for which to make amends.

He turned to go.

"And Sawyer?"

He paused.

"Godspeed on this journey God has for you, my friend. Godspeed."

Chapter Four

Honey peered through the cord grass across the shallow drifts of the channel that separated the barrier island wildlife refuge from her home.

A gentle low tide lapped against the end of the canoe she and Max had beached on a high spot of muck and mud. Migratory birds on their yearly autumnal stopover cawed above her head. The blue-green waters waxed and waned according to the tide and the pull of the moon. Reflecting the ebb and flow of her life, too.

Uninhabited islands protected the peninsula from the fierce Atlantic currents and storms. And beyond the dunes where once a fishing village and lighthouse thrived, ocean waves churned. As did her emotions since Sawyer Kole strolled into her life again.

The soothing in and out rhythm of the tide mirrored the sum total of their relationship. Only not so soothing. More like choppy, unpredictable and treacherous.

Suddenly, Max gave a shout.

Jolting, her heart flatlined. She'd taken her eyes off him for one moment, but that's all it took. Knee-deep in the murky water and her feet encased in layers of marsh mud, she spun a one-eighty almost toppling over when she lost her balance.

But five yards away, Max—too springy to be constrained by mere mud—bounced on the balls of his feet. He cupped his small hands around his mouth. "Aunt Honey! Look!" He gestured toward a kayak rounding the curve of the not-too-distant shoreline.

The channel sparkled like glittering diamonds in the late afternoon sun. And she'd recognize that blond towhead anywhere. After all, hadn't it nightly haunted her dreams?

Max waved like a signalman on an aircraft carrier. "Ahoy, Coastie!"

Sawyer pointed the nose of the kayak toward the mud bank. Sloshing forward through the ankle-deep mud, Max surged forward to meet him.

Honey remained rooted in place. Unable—as in life—to either move forward or backward. Trapped in the mire that was Before Sawyer Kole, and the bleakness of her life After Sawyer Kole.

She shaded her hand over her eyes as Sawyer leaped sure-footed over the side of the kayak where Mighty Max rushed to help Sawyer drag the kayak to higher ground.

She let out an exasperated sigh. "What are you doing here?"

Like the shy, awkward boy Max had never been, Sawyer jammed his hands into his pockets. "I came looking for you."

"That ship sailed a long time ago, Kole."

He dropped his gaze.

"Why are you really here?"

"I wanted to talk. Ask for your forgive—"

"Save it for someone who cares, Kole. I'm working on forgiveness. Don't push it. Or me."

Her nephew propped his fists on his hips, Super Max-style. "Aunt Honey… Be nice."

She winced, recalling Max's earlier assessment of her at

the diner. Earlier and accurate—at least every time Sawyer Kole got too close.

Giving her a vexed look, Max angled toward Sawyer. "You ever been clamming?"

"No." Sawyer flicked a glance her way. "Don't think we ever got around to—"

"We never got around to a lot of stuff, Kole." Her mouth twisted. "Your choice, remember?"

Max scrabbled inside the canoe. "Got any more of those marsh moccasins, Aunt Honey?"

At Sawyer's quizzical look, Max lifted his suede-clad foot above the waterline. "Aunt Honey makes these. Keeps your feet from getting cut on the clam shells."

Honey curled her lip. "You never know what lurks in the muck. Stub a toe. Slice open a foot. And no, Max. This Coastie only wears cowboy boots, best I recall."

Sawyer blew out a breath. "Honey… I'm sorry. You'll never know how sorry. I only—"

"Don't call me Honey…" She growled.

He raked a hand across his hair, leaving the sun-bleached buzz cut standing on its ends. "Sometimes you make me want to take a long walk off a short pier."

She narrowed her eyes at him. "Yeah, blame the victim."

"I never meant for things to turn out the way they did. Though in the long run—"

"How *did* you mean for things to turn out then, Kole? Better in the long run for you, huh?"

"That's not what I meant." He heaved a breath. "If maybe we could take a drive and—"

She gave him a nice view of her back. "I'm not going anyplace with you."

Max snorted. "Stop being a big baby, Aunt Honey. Come on, Sawyer, I'll teach you how a proper waterman goes clamming."

She glided her feet through the mud, the balls of her feet searching for the rounded shell.

"Just like Aunt Honey's doing, Sawyer. Slide… And dig with your toes."

Honey couldn't resist a look over her shoulder.

"Slide…" Hands behind his back, Max coasted forward in a stride not unlike an Olympic speed skater. "Slide… Slide. You try it, Sawyer."

Max stumbled and then righted himself. "Granddad says I got an eagle eye for finding clams. You gotta look for keyhole shapes in the mud. It's the sign of clams underneath feeding."

Crouching, he plunged his hand beneath the outgoing tide. Scrounging through the mud, seconds later Max raised his arm, a shell clutched in his hand. "Aunt Honey's clam chowder, here we come."

Honey sighed. "You don't have to become one with the mud, Max. We have a spade and rake in the canoe, you know."

"Muddier is better." Max scooted a few inches farther. "Got another one, Aunt Honey." He grinned. "And another one. I hit the mother lode."

Sawyer cut his eyes at her.

Against her will, a smile tugged at her mouth. "He went gold panning on a recent trip to visit Braeden's Alaska hometown."

"Bring the bucket, Sawyer. Get the rake, Aunt Honey."

She laughed. And at the sound, Sawyer's eyes crinkled, the corners fanning out.

Ignoring the heart palpitations his eyes ignited, she slogged toward the neon yellow bait bucket resting next to Sawyer's bare feet and the canoe.

Sawyer motioned toward the words on her T-shirt. "It's a Shore thang that only you, Beatrice Honey Duer, could look beautiful while clamming in a tidal estuary."

He thought she was…? She came to an abrupt stop and lost her balance. Her arms flailing—Sawyer's eyes went big, Max shouted—she landed butt first in the muck. Sinking to her elbows.

Sawyer let out a rumbling belly laugh.

Honey glared at him. "Don't you dare laugh, you landlubbing cowboy." She blew a strand of hair out of her face. "Max! Get over here."

Max hustled over, sending a tsunami of marsh water over her head. She sputtered and coughed. Extricating her hand from the mud, she swiped at a rivulet of water cascading down her nose.

Sawyer smirked.

"What?" Her gaze ping-ponged from a chortling Max to the Coastie.

"You wiped mud all over your face, Aunt Honey."

Honey poked out her lip.

Sawyer crossed his arms over the broad muscular chest she couldn't help noticing and rocked on his heels. "I hear women pay big money for a mud bath like this. And you got yours for free, Eastern Shore-style."

Honey muttered something under her breath about she'd show him Eastern Shore-style. Max flung out a hand. Her tug threw Max off his feet.

"You're too heavy, Aunt Honey." He shot a mischievous glance Sawyer's way. "Too many Long Johns, I reckon."

"Max!" she yelled.

Her nephew snickered. "Too many Long Johns. Get it, Sawyer?"

Sawyer unsuccessfully attempted to keep the mirth off his face.

"Help me, Max. I can't get up."

Max let go of her. "She's fallen and she can't get up." He made exaggerated bug on its back motions.

Sawyer extended his hand. "I'll help you, Honey." He flashed her a snarky smile. "I mean, Bee-ahh-triss."

Fluttering her eyelashes at him, she wrapped both her hands around his.

And at his sudden, wary look, she yanked Sawyer forward into the marsh. Fighting to right himself without landing face first, he landed with a plop beside her. Mud particles flew in every direction, including her Shore Thang shirt.

Okay… Maybe not the best idea.

Especially when, taking his cue from the grown-ups, Max belly flopped between them. Brackish water blasted over both Honey and Sawyer.

"Max!"

"Dude!"

Cupping his hand, Sawyer funneled a wave of water in Max's direction. Grinning, Max splashed back.

"Stop it, Max." She struggled to pry herself from the muck. "And Sawyer, stop egging him on. Will the two of you look at what you've done to me?" Honey plucked a long strand of sea grass out of her hair.

Max clasped his arms around Sawyer's neck. "We ought to do this more often, Aunt Honey."

She grunted.

With the boy dangling off his back, Sawyer staggered to his feet. "I agree, Beatrice. Why don't you?"

Always particular about her appearance, she wrinkled her nose at the reeking odor of marsh mud at low tide. "Because we're going to have to hose off the canoe, not to mention us, when we get to the dock."

"Yahoo!" Max fist-pumped the air. "No bath tonight."

"That's not what I said, Max."

At the sandbar, Max slithered off Sawyer's back like an eel.

Sawyer flicked a daub of mud off the boy's cheek. "Try

to de-sludge yourself as much as you can, Max, before getting into the canoe, okay?"

And once again venturing into the water, Sawyer offered his hand to her. "You pull off gorgeous even if you are covered in slime."

"Trusting soul, aren't you? Who's to say I won't pull you in again?"

"Who's to say I'm not hoping you'll do exactly that?"

The Oklahoma drawl of his sent a tingle down her spine. Cheeks burning, she grasped hold of his hand.

Both feet planted, he pulled. And with a squelching, sucking sound, he extracted her from the muddy tomb.

He stepped back a pace, giving her breathing room. "Thanks for trusting me."

She scowled. "Forgiveness is one thing. Trusting is another. Trust has to be earned one day at a time."

"I'd like the chance to earn back your trust. We were friends… Before."

Before. Always before. She was so sick of Before.

"Thought you were shipping out next week after Labor Day. Your eight-second, bronco-busting attention span kicking into gear again? Takes more than a hand up to earn trust, Coastie."

"Well, you know what they say?" His lazy cowboy grin buckled her knees. "Got to get right back on the horse that threw you."

"Did you just compare me to a horse, Kole?"

"Mule-headed is more like it." He retreated toward the kayak when she reached for a glob of mud. "How about I follow you to the lodge?"

"How about you keep paddling toward England?"

"Aboot." He pursed his lips, imitating the lilting local cadence. Sawyer gave her a wicked grin. "You know how I love it when you Shore-talk me, baby."

With as much dignity as she could muster, she pushed the canoe off the mud and held it for Max to climb aboard. "Don't call me baby. I'm nobody's baby. Not Dad's. Not Amelia's. And definitely never yours. Steady, Max," she instructed as she joined him in the canoe.

Max grabbed hold of both sides as the canoe rocked until she evenly distributed their weight.

"What *aboot* your clam bucket, Beatrice?"

She thought aboot—*about*—cracking the paddle over his cocky Coastie head until she remembered the eight-year-old eyewitness and her responsibility to be the grownup. "For the love of fried flounder, just hand me the bucket, Kole."

"Your wish is my command." He waded in and positioned the plastic bucket between her feet and Max.

"That'll be the day."

After shoving off in the kayak, Sawyer pulled alongside their canoe.

"Even strokes, Max." She congratulated herself on the tremendous willpower she exerted in averting her eyes from the play of muscle along Sawyer's bicep. "Paddle on the right, Max. I'll take the left."

And then Sawyer started singing an old Irish sea shanty her dad used to sing to her when she was a little girl. A song called "Holy Ground."

"Fare thee well, my lovely Dinah,
a thousand times adieu.
We are bound away from the Holy Ground
and the girls we love so true.
We'll sail the salt seas over
and we'll return once more,
And still I live in hope to see
the Holy Ground once more.

You're the girl that I adore,
And still I live in hope to see
the Holy Ground once more."

It annoyed Honey to no end that by the chorus Max matched his stroke to Sawyer's rollicking cadence. Yet at the sound of his mellow baritone, she worked hard to keep from smiling.

"Oh now the storm is raging
and we are far from shore;
The poor old ship she's sinking fast
and the riggings they are tore.
The night is dark and dreary,
we can scarcely see the moon,
But still I live in hope to see
the Holy Ground once more.

You're the girl that I adore,
And still I live in hope to see
the Holy Ground once more."

He had a right nice voice. Not that she'd ever tell him that. Would only enlarge that already swelled ego of his. She reminded herself of the fleeting nature of cowboy Coastie charms.

But in no time flat, they arrived at the Duer dock. Sawyer scrambled out of the kayak and hoisted Max onto dry land. Beaching the canoe onto the shore, Sawyer offered his hand again. "Beatrice."

Honey was already wishing she'd never told him to call her that. But she placed her hand in his, unsure if she'd receive a dunking or not. However, he set her feet onto solid ground and released her hand immediately. But not before she noted how his hand trembled at her touch.

And something knotted a long, long time, started to uncoil within Honey.

Clambering onto the dock, he cranked the faucet and freed the hose wound around a piling. "Max, your turn first."

Max shivered in his cut off jeans and Chincoteague Pony Roundup shirt. He shimmied when the cold spray of water hit his head. Sawyer kept the nozzle trained on Max's short crop of hair until the curls resumed their natural carrot-topped hue. Bobbing on his tippy toes, Max closed his eyes as Sawyer spray washed his face, neck and clothes.

A brown puddle formed at Max's feet. "Look at the dirt coming off me, Aunt Honey. Cool."

She grimaced. "And thanks to you both, I've got mud caked in places I don't want to think about."

Aboot... She flushed as Sawyer rolled his tongue in his cheek.

"I'd leave that go if I were you, Kole. Max, get the bucket out of the canoe and then you're in charge of cleaning the canoe and the paddles."

A gust of wind buffeted Braeden's sailboat, the *Seas the Day*, tied at the slip on the other side of the dock. Shuddering in his wet clothes, Max grabbed the clam bucket. "I'll take these to the kitchen and be right back."

"You better," she called after Max, disappearing up the path to the house. "Granddad will have your head if you don't make sure the equipment is clean."

Sawyer held up the nozzle. "Your turn to come clean, Beatrice."

Honey gave him her best put-a-Coastie-in-his-place look. "I don't need your help."

Sawyer smiled. "Thing is, I'm learning everyone needs help from time to time."

Honey turned the hose on herself. "Not from you, I don't." She shut her eyes and allowed the water to trickle over her head, neck, shirt and shorts. She opened her eyes to find Sawyer studying her with an unwavering focus.

"What?" she grunted.

"You missed a spot—several huge chunks in fact—in your hair."

Honey tilted her head over the side of the pier, her hair dangling over the tidal creek. She ran the hose water and her hand through her shoulder-length hair. "Am I good now?"

"From where I stand, you always look good. But no, you've still got mud in that hard to reach place on the crown of your head. Here." He reached for the hose. "Let me."

She eyed him for a second before surrendering the hose. He gave her a crooked smile meant to reassure. Instead, it curled her toes and jump-started her pulse.

"Lean your head..." Sawyer directed the stream of water and finger-combed the mud out of the strands of her hair. "Good. Stay like that. There..."

At his touch, she squeezed her eyes shut and reminded herself to breathe. In and out. Like Sawyer appeared in her life. Here today—

"Okay. I think I got it."

Eyes wide open and with tingles frolicking like dancing dolphins across her skin, she realized he hadn't stepped away. But he dropped his hand with the hose to his thigh. And his free hand?

It still lingered, woven into the locks of her hair.

Only inches away, his eyes had gone a smoky blue. She took a quick breath. He cradled the nape of her neck and drew her closer.

In the circle of his arms, she soaked in his warmth. He tilted his head. Her lips parted.

"Honey!"

She jerked. Sawyer stepped back.

Amelia waved from the screened porch. "Honey! Sawyer!"

"She shouldn't be on her feet. Doctor's orders."

But Amelia came down the steps and let the screen door bang shut behind her. Sawyer turned off the faucet and recoiled the hose.

"What's wrong?" Honey surged forward, clasping Amelia's sleeve. "Did the contractions return? Do we need to take you to the hospital?"

Amelia shook her head. "No. I'm fine. But Braeden called. Thought Sawyer might be here." A smile lifted her cheeks. "Turns out he was right."

Sawyer's posture altered, becoming all business. "Is there a problem at the station?"

Amelia moistened her lips. "Braeden's calling for the off-watch Station Kiptohanock crew to report to headquarters. The forecast's changed. The tropical depression skipped tropical storm status and mushroomed into Hurricane Zelda."

"What's its current status?" Sawyer frowned. "And where is it projected to make landfall?"

Amelia took a deep breath. "It's Category 4 and gaining speed. Braeden's meeting now with Accomack County Emergency Management officials to coordinate strategies. Landfall is estimated to occur somewhere between Hatteras and Ocean City."

Worry prickled Honey. "Putting the Shore right in the middle of its path."

"Like a bull's-eye." Sawyer's mouth tightened. "Increasing our chances for major storm damage."

"What about the Decoy Festival this weekend? Has it been cancelled?"

"The storm's headed our way, but not till later this week. So for now, the festival's still a go." Amelia swallowed.

"But it's going to get bad. Maybe mandatory evacuations if it truly veers in our direction."

Honey sniffed. "Real Shoremen don't leave because the wind changes direction. We stand our ground."

"It's a bad wind that never changes." Amelia gave Honey a pointed look. "And I'm not just talking about a hurricane."

Sawyer's brow furrowed into a V. "If the Coast Guard tells you to go, you better go." He surveyed his mud-splattered clothing. "Good thing I keep a spare uniform in my vehicle."

Come to think of it, she'd have known Sawyer was back in town if she'd spotted that flashy blue convertible of his.

Honey flicked him a look. "You better hose off first, Coastie, or you'll ruin your fancy car."

"Sold it. Got me a truck like I had in Oklahoma."

Avoiding her gaze, he headed toward the dock once more. "I better get moving. Cool off while I'm at it, too."

Him and her both.

But a truck? Sawyer Kole had a truck?

She wondered why he'd made the change. Wondered what the change signified about him. Maybe more in keeping with his true cowboy nature?

From the house, Max bellowed for Mimi. Amelia trudged uphill, leaving Honey staring after Sawyer's broad-shouldered back.

Because most of all, Honey wondered why in the name of flying Long Johns she still cared.

Chapter Five

Labor Day weekend was always busy for the small boat station, even without a hurricane bearing down on the Eastern Shore.

Sawyer had spent the past twenty-four hours on patrol, boarding and citing a plethora of recreational boats on this last official weekend of summer. Citations included reckless endangerment due to excessive speed in the harbor and/or alcohol, which didn't mix with driving a boat any more than it did with driving a vehicle. Too many vessels also lacked mandatory safety equipment—like life jackets—on board.

Midday Saturday word came of a collision out in the channel beyond the Kiptohanock marina. Sawyer and his crew launched the twenty-four-foot Special Purpose Shallow Water craft and arrived on the scene ten minutes after the call. They found two mangled Jet Skis dead in the water.

A charter captain Sawyer recognized from the Sandpiper had witnessed the accident and called it in. The captain and several other good Samaritans who'd stopped to offer assistance dog-paddled in the water near the wreckage tending to the injured. Sawyer came alongside with the rescue boat.

"One Jet Ski carried a single rider." The captain kept a firm grip on an unconscious man in his early twenties floating on his back. "The other ski contained two. A male and female."

The crew pulled the more injured man from the water immediately. Reaves went to work on the unresponsive jet skier. Sawyer and Wiggins secured the remaining two college-aged kids on board. The female clutched her arm like a broken bird wing to her chest.

"Make sure EMS is waiting on the dock," Sawyer instructed. "Reaves?"

On her knees bending over the first victim, she shook her head. "He's breathing. I put a neck brace on him, but I suspect some degree of head injury. We need to get him to shore like yesterday."

"Roger that." With all souls accounted for and safely aboard, Sawyer hit the throttle and chugged the boat toward Kiptohanock.

The waves were choppy, though the incoming storm was still well out to sea somewhere off the Carolina coast. Like him, the crew felt the tension, their nerve endings thrumming at the palpable change in the air. Urgency mounted in Sawyer's chest to get the injured to shore while not jarring any more than necessary the unconscious man, who might also have spinal injuries.

It was with a great deal of relief he steered the response boat into the harbor. The whirling lights of the Accomack County ambulance provided a welcome sight. Wiggins threw the mooring lines to Dawkins on the station pier. Sawyer helped Reaves off-load their patients into the capable hands of the paramedics.

Sawyer glanced toward the square where the Duck Decoy Festival appeared to be in full swing. Non-native come-heres, born-heres and been-heres thronged the green space. Vendors sold a variety of fast food options. The smell of popcorn and clam burgers teased his nostrils. His stomach rumbled.

Reaves laughed. "A long time since breakfast, XPO?"

Sawyer scrubbed his hand over his face. "What breakfast? I'm talking since dinner last night."

Braeden met them at the station entrance. "If you don't drift far, your crew could take a long overdue break."

Sawyer scrutinized his crew. Weariness showed on their faces. It was going to be a long weekend. And with the hurricane on the horizon, rest would be a commodity none of them could afford even after the crowds went home late Sunday.

"I'll finish up here. Go ahead and fill your bellies." Sawyer scanned the square. His eyes roamed past the post office, library, cafe and boat repair shop. "Better get it while you can. But the chief's right, keep an ear out in case we catch another call."

Wiggins heaved a huge sigh. "Funnel cake here I come."

Reaves adjusted her headgear. "That's what I'm talking about. That and some foot-long hot dogs."

Friendly bantering ensued as the junior guardsmen moved toward the food trucks lining the sea wall. Of their own volition, Sawyer's eyes zeroed in on Honey manning a table near the gazebo. A line had formed where she sold tickets to a race involving rubber ducks. His pulse accelerated watching the sea breeze lift and tangle the tendrils of her hair.

She laughed at a remark from one of the come-heres in line. His gut tightened. There was so much he wanted to say to her—needed to say to her—but couldn't.

Despite what her family believed, he'd decided after their near fatal—to his heart—romantic collision on the Duer dock the other day, perhaps it'd be best for him to keep his head down, nose to the Coastie grindstone for the duration. And once the hurricane threat, God willing, petered out next week, ready himself for the Outer Banks assignment Braeden had promised in North Carolina.

Or at least that's what Sawyer told himself every hour on the hour since he'd last spoken to Honey. With effort, he forced his mind back to the job at hand.

He angled toward the station. Away from temptations to his resolve like food and Honey. Though not necessarily in that order. "I'll take care of the paperwork, Chief."

"First things first, Petty Officer. Rubber duck race commences this afternoon."

Sawyer paused, his hand on the station door.

"This station has always had a respectable finish at the rubber duck race." Braeden flicked a languid glance his way. "I'm sure I don't need to remind you that part of the XPO's job at Station Kiptohanock is community relations and maintaining goodwill between the local populace and the Guard."

Sawyer tensed, unsure where this was headed. "Yes, Chief. I would never damage the stellar relationship the station enjoys with the village."

Braeden folded his arms across his chest. "That being said, on the other hand, we have a reputation to safeguard. An illustrious race history to preserve. Coastie pride to—"

"If you're trying to get me over to Honey's booth, I think that's a bad idea, Chief." Sawyer frowned.

Braeden rocked back on his heels. "Wasn't aware you'd been promoted over my head, Kole." His brown eyes hardened. "Wasn't informed you called the shots around here. Or that your personal agenda topped station business."

Sawyer went into regulation stance. "No, Chief. Not at all, Chief."

"Then I suggest you cease and desist from your pity party and get out there and lead from the front. Set the example for the crew. We've got a race to win. You've got to get out there and play if you want to win, Kole. On all fronts. Professional and personal."

"She's made it real clear about how she feels about me."

His cheeks heated thinking how close he'd come a few days ago to kissing Honey before Amelia interrupted. He'd promised himself he wouldn't touch, much less kiss, her. But Honey had a curious effect on his best intentions. Like the surf eroding sand castles on the beach.

Sawyer ought to be glad Amelia had intervened. Saved them from disaster. Him, from drowning in something that could never be. Although in contemplating Death by Honey, his heart thudded. What a way to go.

But still a question intruded in his rare moments of downtime since. The question of how Honey would've responded if he'd lost what was left of his mind and actually kissed her.

Would she have slapped him silly? Or—his mouth went dry—kissed him senseless?

"Are you listening to me, XPO?" Braeden's tone snapped Sawyer back to reality. "Or must I add dereliction of duty to the charges you seem to accrue on your record every time you and Honey Duer get within ten feet of each other?"

Sawyer swallowed. "Perhaps why it'd be better if Wiggins or Reaves or—"

"That's an order, Petty Officer." Braeden clenched his teeth. "If nothing else, it's time to take one for the team, Kole. There's a race to be won. Unless a big call comes in, until further notice, you're on duck duty."

At rigid attention, Sawyer focused his gaze on the air space above Braeden's right shoulder. "Aye, aye, Chief."

"I can't take much more of Honey's Dr. Jekyll and Mr. Hyde routine at home." Braeden softened his tone. "She's been surly, alternating with mopey, ever since you were out there the other day."

Sawyer cut his eyes at Braeden. "I bring out the worst in her, Chief."

"You bring out the stubborn in each other." Braeden blew out a breath. "And I'm guessing you haven't yet explained what happened three years ago."

"I tried to apologize, but she's not interested in my lame excuses. Fact is, I walked away from her. From the best thing that's ever come into my life. We were so..." Sawyer bit his lip. "I can't blame Honey for wanting nothing to do with me. I don't deserve—"

"Stop with the deserving," Braeden growled. "I don't deserve Amelia. Or Max in my life, either. Much less this chance to be a father in my own right. None of us deserve anything but for the grace of God."

Braeden gripped Sawyer's shoulder. "And the real fact is, you're like the brother I never had."

Sawyer tightened his jaw to keep it from quivering.

"I'd love for Honey to make you my brother officially. We all feel that way. We all want you in the family."

Sawyer cocked his head. "Everyone except for Honey."

Braeden raked his hand over his head. "It's neck and neck on who's going to win Most Hardheaded between the two of you. Honey with her carefully constructed pretense of indifference or you with your determination to punish yourself."

"Respectfully, Chief—"

"Respectfully, Kole, I'm ordering you to get over there and buy a rubber ducky. Or two. Or—" Braeden poked a finger in Sawyer's chest. "However many it takes to win the race. It's time for you to get creative, XPO. And I'm not just talking about the race, either."

"Creative?" Sawyer scowled. "What does that mean?"

"It means it's time to use that head of yours for something more than a hat rack for Coastie headgear. Time to crank the smile Honey finds irresistible up a notch."

If only…

"Time to make a date and work that incredible Coastie charm you wielded to such tremendous effect three years ago." Braeden tilted his head. "The legendary charm you hide behind. The same charm with which you reel 'em in."

"I'm out of the reel 'em in business. Not since Honey."

"Then I suggest—no, I strongly *advise*—you get to work. Winning not just the hearts and minds of Kiptohanock, but more especially one Beatrice Elizabeth Duer. You roger that, XPO?"

He clicked his heels together and gave Braeden a salute. "Loud and clear, Chief." He grimaced. "Loud is exactly what happens every time we get too close. Better prepare yourself for fireworks. Explosions."

"*Semper paratus*, Kole." Braeden smirked. "Always Ready, after all, is the Coastie motto."

Right. Famous last words. He'd confronted drug lords and human smugglers on the high seas with less trepidation than facing the beautiful Hostess with the Mostest.

Sawyer took a deep breath before plunging into the midst of the Decoy Festival hordes. Saying a brief, but sincere, prayer. And gathered the remnants of his almost-forgotten swagger.

Time to cowboy up.

Chapter Six

"Rubber duckies can be adopted for five dollars each. The race starts at three this afternoon."

A gentle sea breeze blew a strand of hair against Honey's face, caressing her cheek. Stationed at the gazebo on Kiptohanock's square, she pointed to the black-lettered number inked on the duck's backside. "At the end of the race, winners will be announced by their racing number. So don't forget to cheer for your ducky. All proceeds benefit the Waterman's Association Widows and Orphans Fund."

She handed the bright yellow duck across the table to a couple from Ohio whose info she'd recorded on the roster. "Lucky number 143 for you. And your entry also qualifies you to take part in the Best Decorated Ducky contest."

"You'll find supplies to decorate your ducky over there." She gestured toward the volunteer-manned tables positioned throughout the square. "Decorated duckies must be ready for judging by 2:00."

Max attached a paper wristband with the ducky's corresponding number to the wife's hand.

Honey handed the husband the printed flyer. "You must be present to win the race and/or contest. Prizes include a half day charter fishing trip courtesy of the *Now I Sea*, a free day's rental of kayaks from Kiptohanock Outfitters, a dozen Long Johns from the Sandpiper Cafe and an excursion aboard Senior Chief Scott's personal sailboat, *Seas the Day*."

"That's my dad's boat," Max informed them.

Honey gave the come-heres a wide smile. "Welcome to Kiptohanock."

She surveyed the busy waterfront and the tourists thronging the Duck Decoy Festival. Fingers crossed, Hurricane Zelda would swerve into the open Atlantic and blow itself out next week without damage to people or property. This festival brought the come-heres and locals out in full force.

Hopefully, this last weekend of summer would benefit everyone's bottom line. The professional duck decoy carvings had been judged in the town hall this morning. And the grand prize winner won a two-night stay at the Duer Lodge.

At a sudden gust of wind, she tucked an errant tendril behind her ear. The wind had picked up—courtesy of Hurricane Zelda—and the waves in the harbor were choppy. Great for the upcoming duck race. The committee always bought the ever-upright duckies. Guaranteed to never go topsy-turvy in the water, they delivered the best show for duck race enthusiasts.

The orange-and-blue flag of the Coast Guard fast response boat appeared in the distance where the harbor widened into the channel. She'd watched the crew empty out of the station an hour earlier in response to a distress call. Careful to stay attentive for their return. Not because she'd spotted Sawyer heading the mission, but because…

She fiddled with the pearl stud at her ear. Because as a patriotic American citizen she was concerned for every member of the Guard's well-being.

Right. She tore her gaze away—with effort—from the

activity on the Coast Guard dock as the fast boat edged into the slip. As a distraction, she focused on Amelia—allowed out for good behavior today—manning one of the decoration booths. Max, bored with money transactions, spotted the little redheaded girl and headed off to terrorize her.

Despite Honey's best intentions, her gaze wandered once more toward the station pier as Sawyer stepped over the gap and helped a Coastie secure the mooring lines to the cleats on the pier.

Stop it.

Honey shifted her gaze to the Sandpiper, where her father jawed with his ROMEO—Retired Old Men Eating Out—compatriots over lunch. Although her father was hardly old. Late fifties. And since recovering from his heart attack a few years ago, full of vim and vigor.

Sometimes too much vim and vigor. Honey's mouth pursed, recalling the lecture she'd received following The Battle of the Long Johns.

Honey had no idea what had possessed her to act in such an unladylike, unHoneylike fashion. Actually, she did know. Sawyer Kole. And after what almost happened on the Duer dock a few days ago?

She blushed and buried her head in the rubber duck roster. Exactly why she planned to avoid the Coast Guard petty officer at all costs. She had an image to maintain. "Fool me once," she muttered to no one in particular.

A shadow fell across the clipboard. Her eyes lifted to find her Coastie nemesis, arms crossed, smirking at her across the table. She bit back a sigh. Avoidance not so easy a feat in a town the size of Kiptohanock.

"What do you want, Kole?"

The smirk only widened. "After our recent close encounter, you really want to go there, Beatrice?"

"I'm busy." She waved her hand toward the harbor. "Don't you have somebody to rescue?"

"Taking in the festival ambience." He cocked his head. "But a guardsman's work is never done. Always prepared. Always ready. And there's all kinds of rescues, I've found."

Honey made a face. "Well, no damsel in distress here. You'd best be on your way and quit holding up the line for paying customers."

Sawyer made an elaborate show of glancing over both shoulders. "Doesn't appear I'm holding up anyone. Besides, I am a paying customer. Or at least, I will be." He stuck his hand in his operational duty uniform pockets. "The Coast Guard station always contributes a ducky representative."

Honey made sure he observed her curl her lip. "The Duers have been Kiptohanock Duck Race Champions five years in a row. Not to mention," she flicked a look toward the tables laden with art supplies, "Best Decorated Ducky three seasons running."

Sawyer arched his brow. "Are you challenging the Guard's seamanship, Beatrice?"

Honey strained forward over the table. "A Duer duck will win out over you puddle pirates anytime, any race."

Sawyer got in her face. "You want to make a personal contest between you and me that Coastie Duck outperforms Duer Duck in the race?"

His breath fanned her cheek. Her heart accelerated at an old memory of the taste of his lips on hers. Mint. Her throat constricted. But she couldn't back down now. "You're on."

Sawyer extended his hand.

After the stunt she'd pulled in the marsh, she eyed his hand with trepidation. He dared her with his eyes. She took his hand, steeling herself against the goose pimples going up and down her arm from the heat of his skin.

Sawyer squeezed her fingers. "So what do I win when I win?"

"You're not going to win, Kole. I told you that." She tried easing out of his handclasp.

He held on, refusing to let go. "Oh, no. Not so fast, Beatrice."

"You mean when *I* win, Kole."

"How about we make this interesting? If the Guard wins, you supply the station with a week's worth of desserts. And as for me, Girly-Girl?"

She rolled her eyes. "Stop calling me that."

"You said not to call you *baby* or Honey. So Girly-Girl it is." He continued, undeterred. "And when I win, Girly-Girl, I want an evening of your time."

"A date?" she sputtered. "Of all the—" She growled. "Not going to happen."

"Scared, Beatrice?

Honey yanked her hand free. "I'm not scared of you."

"Then what's the problem? If you're so sure you're going to win anyway." He gave her that slow, devastating smile. "And if you do somehow manage to win, what would you claim as your prize?"

She narrowed her eyes. "*When* I win, I'll still supply a week's worth of desserts to my brother-in-law's crew in appreciation for Coastie service to this nation. But you'll..."

Honey jabbed her finger at his Coastie-clad tropical blue chest. "You'll... You'll..." She cast her gaze around the town square, grasping for the worst possible punishment to inflict on the oh-so-cocky Coastie.

"I'll what?"

Honey clenched her jaw. "You'll have to clean the toilets, make the beds and wash the laundry for a week at the lodge."

Sawyer, to her fury, grinned.

Honey floundered. "Wearing the frock-saver of my choice..."

"I've been told I look good in pink," Sawyer teased.

"Under my constant supervision..." she snarled.

Sawyer rocked on his heels. "Either way, a win-win for me. Getting to spend time with you."

Honey pounded the table with her fist. The money box rattled. "We'll see how perky you feel after scrubbing toilets, Kole." She thrust the signup roster at him. "Five dollars."

Sawyer pointed to the poster tacked to the front of the table. "I want one of those special Quack Packs to increase my chances of winning."

Honey bared her teeth. "You'll need every advantage you can get against the Duer Ducks."

"Exactly how many ducks have the Duers entered into the race?"

She lifted her chin. "We lead by example, Kole. You qualify for the Quacker Package with the purchase of twenty ducks."

"The Guard always goes above and beyond. How aboot..." His lips quirked, pausing to make sure she'd caught his Shore inflection.

Honey glared.

Sawyer pulled out a handful of cash from his cargo pants. "How about I adopt thirty ducks since this is for a worthy cause?"

Her mouth dropped as he unrolled and counted fifteen tens. "A hundred and fifty dollars?" she squeaked. "Are you crazy?"

"Nothing else to spend my money on for three years." He shrugged. "And that date night, Beatrice Duer," the look he gave her liquefied Honey's insides. "I aim to win."

Her heart pounding, she tied the wristband around his sun-darkened forearm. "Must you always be so annoying, Sawyer Kole?"

Sawyer placed both palms flat and leaned across the

table, his nose inches from hers. “Must you always be so beautiful, Beatrice Duer?”

Honey made an elaborate show of stuffing the ducks into three grocery bags so he could transport them to the craft table.

“Why I believe that may be the prettiest shade of pink I’ve ever seen rising from beneath the collar of your shirt, Girly-Girl.”

Honey was beginning to understand why Amelia nearly harpooned Braeden in a case of mistaken identity. She’d like to harpoon Sawyer. No case of mistaken identity necessary. He was as annoying as the south end of a mule.

Sawyer stepped back a pace, correctly reading the expression on her face, she figured. Too bad.

“If twenty ducks is the Quacker Package,” he drawled in his husky voice. “What does that make me with thirty? The Biggest Quack of all?”

She gave him a pointed look. “Truer words were never spoken.”

He laughed. “See you at the finish line.”

Arms laden, he winked at her. “And may the best seaman ducky win, Beatrice.”

Sawyer raised the trophy high over his head. The Guard contingent cheered, as did the other participants in the Best Decorated Ducky contest. Except for Honey. Her face seemed frozen in a perpetual scowl of disapproval.

He scanned the artistically accessorized rubber ducks on display. The bride and groom ducks presented by the future newlyweds getting married at the lodge tomorrow. The princess ducks contributed by the local Girl Scouts. The Biblical ducks from the youth group at the church.

Sawyer especially liked the Jonah duck with the hand-lettered sign attached around its neck, Big Fish Beware.

Max’s need-for-speed NASCAR racing duck had tied

for first place in the children's category. Posing for the official photograph, Max and the little redheaded girl, daughter of a former Coastie commander, glowered at each other across the shared billboard-size coupon for a dozen Long John donuts.

Between calls, the crew had made short work of decorating the thirty Coastie ducks. In honor of puddle pirates everywhere, Reaves created several swashbuckling ducks. And there was the authentic, tropical blue Coastie-inspired duck with anchor insignia. Thanks to Seaman Donovan's graphic artist abilities, that duck secured third place in the adult category. Much to Honey's ire.

The Duer ducks—in various renderings of fisherman Seth, artist Amelia and sailboater Braeden—placed in the top ten. Sawyer loved Honey's personalized duck—so girly-girl with the stylish blond-brown wig and fake eyelashes. A strand of fake pearls dotted the duck's neck.

With pearl studs in the approximate location of ears, the Honey Duck was attired in an exact replica of the shirt Honey sported today. The black-and-white polka-dotted frock painted on the duck's midsection certainly made it a standout. Earning the duck and Honey a respectable runner-up to Sawyer's own first place winning Cowboy Duck.

He'd epoxied a tiny braided lasso to his Stetson-clad duck. And taut with chagrin, the ever-stylish Honey fumed and tapped her Keds on the pavement.

Sawyer cocked a hand around his ear. "Is that the gnashing of pearly white teeth I hear, Beatrice?"

"I'd like to gnash..." Her hair glimmering in the afternoon sunlight, she poked out her lips. "Just you wait till race time, Kole. You'll be eating my ducky waves."

He mock-fluttered his lashes. "Promises, promises."

Making a rude noise, she shoved off toward the wharf.

Sawyer followed at a more leisurely pace. The

ROMEOs—including Seth Duer—were working in conjunction with the Coastie Auxiliary and Watermen's Association. They'd officiate at today's race.

After collecting the race entry ducks in a large trash bag, Seth and the *Now I Sea* would anchor a quarter mile offshore at the starting point of the race. At the blast of the towboat's foghorn, the ROMEOs would dump the plastic contestants overboard between ropes tied to two equidistant poles in the channel.

Ropes on both sides created a V-shaped funnel tied off on the pylons of the dock at the finish line. The lines had been strung through colorful swimming pool noodles to keep the wayward seafaring ducks in bounds. Other volunteers stood poised at the end of the pier with fishing nets to collect the ducks and return them to their "sponsors."

Jaunty flags fluttered in the stiff sea breeze on board dozens of recreational vessels hugging the harbor. Kiptohanockians lined the banks of the town at water's edge. Come-heres and been-heres settled backsides, feet dangling, across the length of the seawall rimming the waterfront of the fishing village.

Max waved to Sawyer just as the little redheaded girl ground a cloud of pink-swirled cotton candy into his face. With a whoop, he set off in hot pursuit, vowing vengeance. Braeden and the girl's father moved to intervene. Sitting in a lawn chair with feet propped up, Amelia threatened to snatch a nautical knot in Max if he didn't stop provoking the little girl. Which prompted outraged howls of protest from injured-party Max.

"You had it coming, Max!" screamed the incensed little redhead.

Commander Weston Clark wrenched his daughter away from doing further harm to Max. Who, likewise, struggled to be free of Braeden's restraining stronghold.

Sawyer smiled. What a family. Never a boring moment around them. He'd have given anything in the world to have the crazy, totally wonderful family Honey took for granted.

Sawyer's gaze went skyward, always attuned to the steeple piercing the Eastern Shore sky. *How I love it here.*

His gaze drifted toward Honey, standing by the volunteer duck wranglers easing into kayaks on the bank. *How I love her.*

And yet today, he'd decided to take a page straight out of Max's playbook. Going with the philosophy that annoying attention was better than no attention at all. What he hoped Braeden would consider "creative."

Yep, Sawyer grimaced, he was a sad, pathetic man. But anything was better than being ignored. Which seemed to be Honey's favorite modus operandi this afternoon.

The walkie-talkie crackled in the mayor's hand. "Ladies and gentlemen duck herders, let me remind you that no attempt to free or interfere with any duck is permitted unless deemed necessary by duck race officials." The mayor gestured toward the water's edge. "Please take your positions."

Sawyer sauntered toward a waiting canoe as other volunteers wrestled their kayaks into the water. One of their responsibilities was to relay play-by-play action to the mayor for rebroadcast, boosting the competitive spirit of the race. He pushed the canoe into the water.

A barefoot Honey waded in behind him. "Where do you think you're going, Kole?"

Sawyer kept a firm hand on the canoe, holding it against the pull of the tide. "With my cowboy expertise, I'm a natural for duck wrangling."

Honey jutted her jaw. "You're a natural to ensure a Coastie duck wins the race, you mean."

Sawyer pretended to wince. "Don't you trust me?"

Ankle-deep in the surf, she planted her hands on her hips. "I wouldn't trust you as far as I could throw you."

He placed a hand over his heart. "I'm crushed."

"No way I'm letting you have an advantage over the Duer Ducks. Where you go, I go."

"Better be careful what you say, Beatrice." He cocked his head. "That sounds kind of matrimonial to me."

She mumbled something under her breath he figured wasn't complimentary.

He swept his arm across the expanse of the canoe. "If you're determined to be my conscience, then be my guest. This puddle pirate never refuses an extra pair of strong arms to row."

Tossing her hair over her shoulder, she stepped into the canoe. He steadied the wobbling boat, making sure she stayed dry while finding her seat. Shoving the water-craft farther off the bank, in one smooth motion he leaped aboard taking the seat behind her.

She glanced over her shoulder and balanced the paddle across her knees. "Ready?"

His mouth curved. "A Coastie is always—"

"Save it, Kole."

Honey dipped the end of the paddle and propelled the canoe forward, through the harbor toward the tidal estuary. And he, with a few periodic dips of his paddle, kept the canoe floating within the zone he'd been assigned, which happened to be nearest to shore.

From the wharf, the mayor shouted through the bull-horn. "On your mark. Get ready. Get set..."

He and Honey hunched in anticipation.

"Go..." yelled the mayor.

The tugboat's horn bellowed across the harbor, signaling the ROMEOs. Seth and his cohorts dumped the ducks into the channel. Hundreds of bright yellow plastic heads bobbed in the waves. From the shoreline, cheers and jeers arose.

"Duck number 409 takes an early lead," the mayor cried.

Armed with walkie-talkies, the other herders kept the mayor and the crowds apprised of the ducks in contention. Equipped with purple pool noodles, the wranglers ensured the ducks didn't get stuck in the lines or in harbor debris.

"Come on, come on." She bounced in the seat. "Go, Lucky 576, go. Go. Go."

Sawyer held on to the sides of the canoe. "Sit still. Or you'll land the both of us in the drink."

"Duck number 324 edges number 576," the mayor announced. A roar erupted from the spectators.

Sawyer grinned. "That's a Coastie duck."

Honey scowled.

Sawyer smacked his lips. "I'm thinking we'll start the evening with dancing—"

Honey grunted. "I'm thinking that's so not happening..."

"It's 576 and 324, beak and beak," shouted the mayor.

The current brought the ducky horde within arm's reach of the canoe. Sawyer reached for one of the purple noodles he'd stashed on board.

She slatted her eyes. "What are you doing?"

He stroked the water with the noodle. "I'm making sure they don't get tangled in the floating seaweed."

"Stop it, Kole." She seized another noodle from between their feet. "You're making waves to ensure Coastie Duck beats Duer Duck."

He sent a ripple of water toward the bobbing ducks. "Like the other wranglers farther out, I'm only making sure the ducks don't stall dead in the water before reaching the finish line."

"You're cheating." She half rose. The canoe tilted.

"I'm not." He frowned and grabbed for the sides. "Sit down, Beatrice."

"You don't get to tell me what to do, Kole." She stood.

He lurched to his feet. "Sit—"

She smacked him in the chest with her noodle. Only his feet planted even with his hips kept him from toppling into the water.

"Beatrice," he hissed. The canoe rocked. "Stop—"

"Prepare to suck seaweed, Coastie. This is so on…" Clutching the noodle, she lunged at him.

Sawyer blocked her jab. "You want it? You got it. Bring it, Duer."

Honey thrust at him again. He parried again. "That the best you can do?"

She whacked the end of her noodle against his. The dull thud of noodle-on-noodle swordplay echoed across the marsh.

"Looks like hostilities have erupted on the sidelines, folks," the mayor commented. Laughter broke out along the shore.

Honey charged at him. He shifted. The canoe tipped. Her arms windmilled. She cried out. He threw himself in her direction to counterbalance.

But too late. The canoe capsized, dumping them both over the side. They landed with a whale of a splash in the waist-deep water. The surge sent the ducks scurrying toward the finish line.

"Number 698 wins!" the mayor shouted.

Sawyer and Honey groaned. Not a Coastie Duck. From the look of her face, he guessed not a Duer Duck, either.

Knees bent, butt in the water, her mouth trembled. Those immaculate white linen trousers of hers weren't so immaculate now. He sighed. How did they keep ending up in this situation? Humiliating each other in front of the whole town.

Swiping a hand over his face, he found his footing. He waited for Honey but knew better than to offer his hand this time. Water dripped from the pearls at her ears and throat. She staggered upright.

Her expression haughty—as haughty as she could be with her hair plastered to her head and water running in rivulets down her ruined clothing—she sloshed toward the bank. After retrieving the canoe, paddles and noodles, he towed the canoe in her wake.

And his gut sank further when he spotted Seth Duer and Braeden Scott waiting for them. Both men's arms crossed, eyes flaming and brows lowered. He plodded toward his doom.

In hindsight, maybe this wasn't the sort of creative wooing Braeden had envisioned. Sawyer had gotten Honey's attention all right. But he reckoned in the long run no attention might prove superior to the wrong kind of attention. Especially when it involved the wrath of Honey's father and brother-in-law.

Chapter Seven

"You either get that girl of your'n under control or…"

Honey's father jerked his chin at his fellow ROMEOs. "Or what?"

The grizzled watermen and retired Coastie auxiliaries lowered their gazes.

Honey darted an angry glance at Sawyer's retreating back. Conveniently for him, he and Braeden had been called to the station with an update on Hurricane Zelda.

Leaving her in the lurch—once again—to face the wrath of the Kiptohanock citizens. How did she get herself into these embarrassing situations with Sawyer?

"Thanks to her," a crusty boat captain jabbed his gnarled thumb in Honey's direction. "First time in the history of the Decoy Festival, a come-here has won the rubber duck race."

She hung her head. A come-here vacationing at one of the resorts near Cape Charles had won. The title lost for Kiptohanock residents till next year. The Duer family's winning streak broken. Surrounded by irate Kiptohanockians, she shifted on the weathered gray planks of the dock.

"That Coastie boy was simply defending himself, the way I see it," Dixie at the diner threw in for good measure.

Honey glared at her former—emphasis on the former—waitress friend.

If it wasn't for the Long Johns, Honey vowed, she'd get the Corner Bakery in Onancock to supply the lodge's pastries from here on out. She sighed. Those Long Johns had been the start of the trouble with her and Sawyer.

Why, oh why, every time she saw him did she feel an overwhelming urge to whack him? It was either that or... She swallowed.

Her father ground his teeth. "I'm well aware who's to blame for this latest fiasco." He cleared his gravelly throat. "And I promise you, it will be dealt with."

"Talk about cowboy Coasties?" He snagged hold of her sleeve. "Somebody's been needing to knock you off your proverbial high horse of haughty for a while now." He tugged her toward his waiting Silverado.

"After the way that Coastie acted—"

"The boy was doing the best he knew how at the time to protect you from himself."

She stopped in her tracks. "What does that mean?"

"Why don't you ask him?" Her father propelled her toward the parking lot. "Though first, I suggest you have a soul-searching chat with your Creator."

Their antics had resulted in disqualifying the Coastie and Duer ducks for behavior unbecoming to waterfowl.

"And you will personally apologize to every member of the Coast Guard station once this weather crisis is over. Then—"

"Isn't that enough?"

Her father flung open the passenger door. "Since Sawyer's personal duck bested yours by a beak, you will honor your commitment to supply pastries to the station house and..."

She threw herself into the suede-upholstered seat.

"And fulfill the terms of your agreement with Sawyer."

Her eyes widened. "You want me to go out with that guy?"

Slamming the door closed, her father glowered through the open window. "I warned you, Honey. If you'd just talk to him, let him explain—"

"Nothing to explain except he's a...a..." Her lips twisted. "Mom taught me not to say words that adequately describe Sawyer Kole."

Seth Duer stalked around to the driver's side. "Your mother would be ashamed—as am I—at the way you're behaving. You're not the only one who's suffered pain. Ever ask the boy about where he grew up? And with whom?"

Honey pivoted in the seat. "What're you talking about? If you're trying to justify his past behavior with some sob story about—"

"Storm's a-coming. I've got a boat to dry-dock." Seth cranked the engine. "And you've got a wedding to orchestrate tomorrow. But after that, baby girl, you've got a date with destiny. A destiny by the name of Sawyer Kole. And one way or the other—easy way or the hard way, take your pick—you're going to settle this thing that's been tearing you apart for over three years."

Honey pursed her lips. "I have no idea what you're talking about. I've barely thought of him in three years."

Seth thrust the gearshift into drive. "Whatever you say, baby girl. But talk to him you will. If nothing else," he headed out of Kiptohanock toward Seaside Road. "You can thank him for his service."

He laughed. The sound without mirth. "Sounds like a long, awkward night to me. But your choice, baby girl. Your choice. You want to stop being treated like a baby? Then grow up, darlin'. Time to grow up."

* * *

"Think the seawall will hold, Chief?"

Wednesday morning, Sawyer took a gander out the station window as concerned Kiptohanock citizens made emergency preparations for the incoming storm.

Lining the seawall assembly-style, the ROMEOs filled sandbags against the storm surge, which would accompany the Category 4 storm barreling up the eastern seaboard.

Braeden took a sip from his coffee mug. "Floyd, Irene, Superstorm Sandy. The Eastern Shore is used to hurricanes and what's usually worse, the flooding. Our problem will be convincing residents to evacuate to higher ground if landfall becomes imminent. They're so used to riding out these storms, their bravery can be misplaced in the event of a worst case scenario."

Hammering filled the air as business owners boarded over windows. The Sandpiper waitresses and owner busied themselves tying down the awning and anything with the potential to become a storm-propelled missile during the high winds sure to come. Reverend Parks staked chicken wire around the church to prevent debris from battering Kiptohanock's small sanctuary.

Dragging his eyes from the white steeple, Sawyer angled, a smile twitching his lips. "So you're saying they'll be stubborn."

Braeden shrugged. "Not a news flash, I know."

"I also want to apologize again about what happened last weekend at the duck race, Chief."

Braeden sighed. "For the record, I'm aware Honey instigated the noodle war. My sister-in-law is nothing if not stubborn. We'll have our work cut out for us convincing the rest of them to leave, too. And then as soon as the winds die down, rescuing the ones who took the chance and lost."

Sawyer scrutinized the plans littering Braeden's desk. "We've done everything we can to prepare before the storm hits. The crew's on alert. We've trained for this. They won't let you down, Chief."

Hurricane Zelda had blazed a path of destruction across the Pamlico Sound of North Carolina before zeroing in on coastal Virginia. Norfolk was prepared for a direct hit, but a cold front nudged Zelda farther east in a direct line toward the Delmarva.

"We'll coordinate our efforts as always with state and local responders. Our mission will be two-fold."

Sawyer nodded. "Protecting people from the sea."

"People come first, but also minimizing the damage to the sea, either manmade or from a force of nature. Environmental concerns always accompany these natural disasters."

"You're thinking about the Katrina rescues, Chief?"

Braeden's lips thinned. "Wasn't old enough to be a guardsman then." He passed a hand over his face as if to scrub away tragic images. "But the Guard was instrumental in saving over thirty-thousand. Possibly our finest hour."

"Finest..." Sawyer grinned. "Yet."

Braeden's mouth quirked. "I'm praying our station never faces anything of that magnitude here in Kiptohanock. And praying the storm downgrades."

"I'll be praying, too." Sawyer cast his eyes skyward to the steeple. "Praying for all of us to survive this current fury."

Watchstander Reaves poked her head inside Braeden's office. "Your wife's on the phone, Senior Chief."

"Thanks." Braeden grabbed the phone and punched On. "Amelia—" He frowned. "What's wrong?"

Sawyer moved forward at the strange note in his voice.

"You're sure?" Braeden's hand white-knuckled the receiver. "They've closed the Bay Bridge Tunnel to traffic due to wind gusts. The hospital here—" A moan echoed.

Braeden's eyes enlarged. "Amelia? Are you all right? Where's your dad?"

Sawyer's heart ratcheted.

"I—I can't leave." Braeden closed his eyes. "All hands are on duty for the duration." A muscle ticked in his jaw.

Sawyer clenched his hands at his sides. Baby Scott couldn't be making his or her entrance at the opening salvo of the worst hurricane to hit the Shore in a generation.

"I'm glad your dad is with you. He'll take you to Riverside. Call me when you get there. Keep me updated." Braeden moistened his lips. "I want to know everything. I wish I could be there..."

Braeden heaved a breath. "I know you understand, but I still wish..." His eyes cut to Sawyer.

Sawyer stepped away into the outer office to give him privacy, but Braeden beckoned for Sawyer to remain.

"I love you, Shore Girl. I'll be praying." Braeden clamped his lips together. "I know you'll be praying for us, too. Bye for now." His hand shook as he replaced the phone into the receiver.

Sawyer's stomach knotted. "Chief?"

But as the chief's training kicked in, Sawyer watched the panic recede from Braeden's eyes and calm leadership take its place.

"She's gone into labor. Full moon tonight, you know." Braeden squared his jaw. "Will make the storm surge worse, too."

"But Amelia's okay?"

"She's in pain and scared. It's too early. Two months too early. The baby..." With studied deliberation, Braeden stacked the scattered papers into a neat pile. "Seth's taking her to Riverside. Can't get to the specialist in Norfolk now. Seth doesn't think they'll make it in time up Highway 13 to Salisbury, either, not with the evacuation traffic."

"You should be there, Chief."

Braeden's mouth tightened. "I have a duty to this station and to Kiptohanock."

If it were Honey—Sawyer gritted his teeth. Honey hated him. Rightly so after he'd made the worst decision of his life and walked away from her.

She'd never carry Sawyer's baby. There'd never be a child. And he only had himself to blame.

"I'm here for you, Chief. I'll man the station. You go—"

Braeden swept his hand across the desk and sent the papers flying. "I'm needed here and you know it."

"What I know is that you're needed at Riverside. With your wife and your baby."

"Amelia understands. We went through the same separation during a typhoon while stationed in Hawaii. And of course, Max decided in the middle of my deployment to require a tonsillectomy." He gave Sawyer a crooked grin.

"Of course, he did, Chief. Sounds exactly like something Max would do."

Braeden laughed. More of a bark really. But a laugh nonetheless.

"And God took care of him just fine, I bet. Amelia Duer Scott is a good Coastie wife. God will take care of her and Baby Scott, too."

"She is a good Coastie wife." Some of the tension eased from Braeden's shoulders. "She puts up with me, doesn't she?"

"Affirmative, Chief." Sawyer gave Braeden a look to let him know he was kidding.

"Right." Braeden regathered the papers. "Back to the hurricane."

Sawyer bent and scooped a few pages, which had fluttered to the floor. "And Honey? She went with them?"

Braeden took the papers from him. "Battening the Duer hatches. Seth told her to evacuate with Max to higher ground. Most of Kiptohanock is relocating to Nandua Middle School. The portmaster has declared Condition Yankee and closed all ports from North Carolina to Maryland. It's going to be a long day."

And it was. With advance winds approaching sixty miles per hour, the station stayed busy rescuing watermen and families who'd not heeded the evacuation directions of the emergency management team.

Between distress calls, Reaves monitored NOAA's weather updates. Sheets of rain fell from the pewter sky over Kiptohanock. Churning waves had obliterated the barrier islands from view.

The tide ran ankle deep along Kiptohanock's main street. Everyone with any sense had holed up on higher ground at the evacuation center. Better fled than dead, Sawyer reckoned.

He pointed to the computer monitor. "High tide looks to coincide with landfall."

Braeden blew out a breath. "Flood stage will reach seven to eight feet at Kiptohanock. Higher in more low-lying areas."

Sawyer grimaced. "Like the Duer Lodge."

The phone rang.

Braeden poured himself his tenth cup of coffee. "Honey's going to be devastated."

"Chief?" Reaves cradled the station phone in her hand. "It's your father-in-law at the hospital."

Braeden shoved the mug at Sawyer and grabbed the phone. "Seth?"

Sawyer, Reaves and the other station crew not currently deployed on search and rescue held their collective breath.

Braeden nodded as if Seth Duer could see him through the phone. "Tell her to hang on. I'll be there as soon as this storm blows over and the situation is stabilized." He clicked off.

"Chief?" Sawyer, as second in command, spoke for them all.

Braeden gave them the first smile he'd sported since the station went on alert and Amelia went into labor. "They stopped the contractions for now. Mother and baby are doing okay. Tough as a sea barnacle, that girl."

Sawyer slapped Braeden on the back. "Baby Scott, too. What else would you expect with such a tough Alaskan and Eastern Shore gene pool, huh?"

Radio static from Sector Hampton Roads drew Reaves. Responding, she raised her eyebrows. "We got another one, Chief. Woman and baby near Oyster trapped by rising water. Climbed out the window onto the roof. Her trailer's almost submerged. No time to call the Jayhawks, even if the helos from Elizabeth City could get into the air."

Sawyer started toward his locker to retrieve his storm gear. "I'll suit up, Chief."

"No," Braeden straightened. "You've been out on the last two calls with no break in between. I'll command the next SAR. Amelia's as situated as she's likely to get. It'll be good to burn off some excess energy and make sure nothing happens to somebody else's baby."

Braeden and the response team had only been deployed ten minutes when Seth Duer called again.

Sawyer intercepted the call. "Mr. Duer, sir?"

"Honey and that blasted house..."

Sawyer frowned. "What's wrong with Honey? Is she all right?"

"I drove to the middle school but no Honey. No Max. She promised me as soon as she stowed the outside equipment, she'd leave."

Sawyer's breath hitched. "You mean she's still at the house? The water's got to be five feet above the shoreline already there." He gripped the phone.

Honey's father growled. "She promised me… It's not like her to endanger Max."

Sawyer pushed down the fear rising in his gut. "I'll take care of it, Mr. Duer. I give you my word. I'll drive over there and bring her back if I have to hogtie her to do it."

"I knew you'd be the man for the job," Seth chuckled, but Sawyer caught the underlying worry in his voice.

Sawyer bit his lip so hard he tasted the metallic tang of his own blood. "I'll call you with a report as soon as we return, sir."

"Appreciate that, son. And Sawyer?"

"Yes, sir?"

"Take care of yourself, too."

Donning his boots and rain slicker, Sawyer trudged toward the rapidly disappearing station parking lot. The weather worsening, time was of the essence. His fury at Honey's stubbornness grew at the same exponential pace as the storm.

The usual fifteen-minute journey on a cloudless day took thirty. At the top of the Duer driveway, he was forced to pull off onto the shoulder of the road.

He'd have to walk from here. Stepping out of the vehicle, he shielded his face from the stinging pellets of water. In shin-deep water, he strained against the increasing force of the wind.

Around the curve of the bent double trees, he spotted the three-story Victorian at last. Although lights shone from within, the house lay completely surrounded by the inlet. Water lapped at the porch steps. If they delayed any longer, Sawyer figured they'd have to swim for it.

Sawyer slogged up the steps, pulling himself upward by sheer brute strength along the railing. Reaching the wide wraparound porch, Sawyer pounded on the door in no mood for any of Honey's histrionics. "Open the door, Beatrice!"

His fist battered the doorframe. "I know you're in there. And you've got five seconds before I'm kicking this door in and coming after you. One..." His boot leveled a blow against the bottom of the door.

"Two..." He pressed his mouth against the glass-paned sidelight of the oak door. "Three..." The door vibrated with another thud from his boot.

Sawyer raised his fist again. "Four—"

"How dare you?" She swung the door wide, leaving Sawyer's hand raised in midair. "What do you think you're doing? This is an antique, you cowboy barbarian."

The wind caught the door, wrenching it from her grasp. The door crashed against the interior wall. She scowled.

He scowled. "*How* dare *you*, Beatrice Elizabeth Duer?"

She arched her brows. "How dare I what?"

He was about done with her snooty high-handedness. "How dare you endanger your life and Coast Guard personnel, whose resources are already stretched thin, because of your frivolous—"

"Frivolous?" Her bellow probably echoed all the way to Delaware. "If I'm so frivolous, why don't you go help somebody who really needs what you have to offer." She jabbed her finger into his slicker. "'Cause I don't need your help, Kole. I've got everything under control."

He leaned across the threshold into her face. "It looks like you got everything under control as you stand ankle-deep in water, Duer."

"All the more reason to stay." She planted her hands on her hips. "Unlike you, I don't walk away and abandon what's important. I need to move everything to the second floor. I've got a lot invested in this lodge. Not to mention it's my home." Her lips quivered momentarily.

Sawyer hardened his heart. "It's not worth your life."

Honey rolled her eyes. "Dramatic much, Kole?"

Sawyer advanced. "That's your department if I remember correctly."

Backpedaling, she folded her arms across her denim shirt. "I've lived through a dozen storms in my lifetime already. A real Shoreman isn't scared of a little wind and rain."

"A real Shoreman ought to have enough sense to come out of the rain, especially hurricane-force rain. This storm isn't like the others. Your father called. I'm here to take you to safety."

Honey actually snorted—as unladylike a gesture as he'd ever seen from the Hostess with the Mostest. "I'm not going anywhere with you. Being with you, I learned the hard way, doesn't equal safety. Not by a long shot."

She hefted a crate of blue pottery and placed it on the stair landing. "But if you're bound and determined to be useful, why don't you grab Daddy's armchair and hoist it up here."

"We're leaving, Beatrice. Now."

She descended the stairs and lifted another box full of checker pieces and beach rickrack.

"You can do this the easy way or the hard way, Beatrice. Your choice."

She spun, her boots making eddying swirls in the water. "When has anything with you been my choice?"

He fought to keep his temper under control. "I don't have time to hash this out with you right now. I'm trying to save your life!" The last part ended with a roar.

She drew back. "I'm not leaving. And you can't make me, Petty Officer Kole." She tipped her chin in defiance.

In two strides, he crossed the living room and plucked the box from her arms. "Watch me." Setting it on the first stair, he grabbed hold of Honey.

Seizing her waist, he slung her over his shoulder. She landed with a whoosh of air on her stomach. She pounded his back and sputtered indignant threats of reprisal. He clamped an arm around her dangling jean legs as she tried to squirm free.

"Let go of me." She pounded her fists on his shoulder blades.

He winced but continued toward the entrance.

"I hate you."

He slogged forward. "Old news, Beatrice."

She yelled at the top of her lungs.

He ignored her. She grabbed hold of the doorframe and hung on. Water had breached the top of the porch.

"Let go, Beatrice. Or I'm going to dump you on your fair derriere right into the Machipongo and let you dog paddle your way to my truck. But one way or the other, you and Max are leaving here."

She stilled. "Max? What are you talking about? He went with Dad and Amelia to the hospital hours ago." She released her hold on the door.

He allowed Honey to slide with a small splash toward the floor. His chest tightened. "Your father said Max stayed here with you. When's the last time you saw him?"

"Max was upset about Amelia being in pain. And about the baby coming. He went looking for the dogs and—" She clapped her hand over her mouth.

"What?"

"I haven't seen Blackie and Ajax in hours, either."

"Animals sense when these things are coming. They tend to burrow somewhere till the worst is over."

Her face went pale. "You don't think he's out there—" she choked off a sob "—searching for them?" She squeezed his arm. "Sawyer, what are we going to do?"

We.

His heart slammed against his rib cage. The first time since he'd returned she'd said his name.

Max's life was at stake. And he wouldn't let her down. Not this time.

"We're going to find him." He locked gazes with her brimming brown eyes. "I promise."

Chapter Eight

Honey blinked back tears. Sawyer called 911 on his handheld radio. Then, he called Reaves at the station.

"They've closed rescue operations till the storm dies down. They can't risk any more lives at this point. They said they'd try to come out once the storm moves off-Shore. But until then..."

She huddled against the railing. "We're on our own."

"Braeden's team isn't back from Oyster yet. The storm's gotten worse fast. They've probably had to take shelter where they could find it."

"We've got to find Max."

Sawyer tightened his jaw. "I'll find Max. No way I'm letting you out in this storm. The wind would knock you clean over."

Honey enfolded her raincoat closer around her body. "I'm tougher than I look. You need me."

Sawyer's sky blue eyes flickered.

Her cheeks burned. "You need my help, I mean."

Sawyer turned away. "I need you to stay here. I can't rescue Max and you, too. Max will be cold and hungry. Best thing you could do is what you do best."

Honey lifted her chin. "What is it exactly you think I do best? I'm more than just some girly-girl."

"Nothing wrong with being a girly-girl. I like girly-girls." Sawyer faced the raw fury of the storm. "Fact is, you strengthen and comfort. You give hope."

He pointed to the tree line. "Maybe Max and the dogs holed up in Braeden's old cabin. I'll check there first."

She caught his arm. "Be careful."

He nodded. "Go back inside, out of the wind and rain." He didn't wait to see if she obeyed.

Which she didn't. She held her breath, afraid the rescuer might need rescuing. Although she hadn't the slightest idea what she could do if worse came to worst.

Under the shelter of the porch, scant though it was, she watched him struggle against the current across what had once been the Duer lawn. Bending almost double, he plowed his way toward the woods and disappeared from view. The minutes ticked by. Her anxiety grew.

Where was Sawyer? How had Max gotten left behind in the shuffle of evacuation? Shame smote her conscience. If she hadn't been so obsessed over saving the inn none of this would have happened.

If anything happened to Max… She clasped her hands under her chin. And if anything happened to Sawyer—

God, please. Help Sawyer find Max. Keep Sawyer and Max safe.

Her first prayer in how long? She squeezed her eyelids shut. *Please, God. Please...*

She sighted a patch of yellow through the trees. She strained forward to see better. His arms wrapped across his chest, Sawyer edged closer in the waist-high water, shielding something—someone—with his body.

A flash of red. Max's mop of carrot curls lay flattened against his skull. Sawyer slipped and stumbled. She gasped. Sawyer recovered and, lips clamped together, persevered toward the porch.

She dashed forward, arms open, to take Max from him. "Max? Is he—?"

Max lifted his head at the sound of his name. His freckles shone in sharp relief against his pale face. "Aunt H-Honey..."

"I got him, Beatrice. I'll take him inside—"

"No," Max squirmed. "Blackie and Ajax, they're still trapped. You got to help 'em, Sawyer."

She tried prying Max's arms from around Sawyer's neck. He clung to the guardsman like a limpet on stone. "Max, come inside. We need to get you warm. Let go of Sawyer."

"Please," Max burrowed his face into Sawyer's shoulder. "Please."

The wind whipped the hood off Sawyer's head. Lines of strain bracketed his mouth. He'd been on call since yesterday. Clamming in the tranquil waters of the inlet seemed ages ago. He had to be exhausted.

"I'll find them, Max." Sawyer unclamped Max's arms and legs from his torso. "I promised you. And I keep my promises."

His gaze shot to hers as if he expected her to argue. "Only way I could get Max to leave the cabin. The dogs are stuck underneath the lattice under the cabin porch."

She pulled at her nephew. "Let him go, Max. You're wasting time Blackie and Ajax may need."

Max reattached his stranglehold to her. She reeled. Sawyer's arms went around her and steadied her from toppling off the porch.

Caught between them, Max's body quivered with cold. She found herself inches from Sawyer's face. The closest in three years to the man who'd never stopped haunting her dreams.

And when he looked at her that way... Her mouth went dry. As if he still...

"I—I wish you wouldn't go back out there. I don't want anything to happen to the dogs. But..." Her heart pounded with fear. "I don't want anything to happen to you, either."

His arms tightened around her and Max. Something raw, something stark, eased in his expression. His lips brushed across her forehead.

She drew a quick indrawn breath.

"I'm tougher than I look." He smiled at his deliberate mimicry of her earlier words. "Take care of Max. Okay?"

Mute, she watched him trudge down what used to be the steps and through the water toward the woods. Her heart torn in two, she forced herself to retreat inside the house. She carried Max upstairs and busied herself by getting him out of his wet clothes and into dry ones. Max insisted on getting into Mimi's bed where he snuggled his cheek against Amelia's pillowcase.

She rummaged through the cardboard box of kitchen supplies she'd carried upstairs before Sawyer arrived. From the thermos of hot water, she fixed a cup of hot chocolate for Max. He practically inhaled the stale Long John donuts left over from breakfast yesterday when the lodge's last guests departed.

Every few moments, however, she rushed to the window, scanning the darkening landscape for signs of Sawyer. He should have returned by now. What was taking so long?

Nightmare scenarios erupted in her mind. Sawyer trapped under the wooden planks of the porch with the dogs. The water rising. The pocket of air diminishing. Sawyer gasping for breath. Going under. Not coming up—

Something yellow bobbed in the fading light. Sawyer... Floundering. His strength giving out. It was a long way to swim. A river of oceanic tide separated him from the house. Two small canine heads dog-paddled beside him.

Honey sucked in a breath and bounded down the stairs.

Sloshing through the knee-deep water, she wrenched open the door. "God, please, help him!" The wind snatched her words away.

She edged as far as she dared on the porch. Two lines tethered the dogs to Sawyer's chest. If one of the dogs were to get snagged on the swirling mass of debris floating past the house, they'd go under and drag Sawyer with them.

"You crazy, stupid man. Let go of them," she hollered into the wind, knowing he couldn't hear.

What was he trying to prove? Risking his life for Max's dogs. Her fear and anger rose. If he didn't drown, she was going to kill Sawyer for scaring her like this.

She clenched her fists. Her head throbbed. His long strokes faltered. Two strokes forward, the wall of water pushed him back three. He was losing ground. He'd never make it.

A shutter tore free from the corner of the porch and flew across the expanse. It smacked Sawyer broadside before careening into the wind. He went under.

Without stopping to think, she dove into the water. She cupped her palms, forcing her body through the churning water. She dodged a lawn chair. She narrowly avoided smashing her head against the battering ram of a downed tree.

She reached Sawyer as a wave broke over his head and dragged him downward. In the semidarkness, she groped for something of him to grab on to. Scissoring her body, she took a deep breath and plunged beneath the water, her arms outstretched searching, seeking—

Encountering something solid, she tugged upward. With a forward thrust, she surged above the surface of the water. She screamed and choked on a mouthful of water as Blackie's coarse wet tongue licked her face.

Not Sawyer. But if Blackie were close, Sawyer had to

be nearby. Somewhere. She splashed the water around Blackie's body. Another whine on her right. Ajax.

Sawyer should be somewhere between them. The line. Treading water to stay afloat, her fist closed around the cord strung between the dogs. Hand over hand, her fingers traced the length of the rope. And was rewarded with the soft, feathery feel of Sawyer's short-cropped hair.

Inserting her arms underneath his shoulders, she rotated him onto his back and rested his head against her shoulder. With Sawyer unconscious, she had to keep his face out of the water. And somehow get them to the shelter of the house.

But her legs were giving out. She wasn't athletic like Amelia. She wasn't going to make it. The distance between the raging ocean bent on reclaiming the Shore as its own and engulfing her home had increased, not lessened.

It was too far. Sawyer was too hurt. They were both going to die. If he wasn't already— *Please, God... No.*

Sawyer groaned. Crying in relief, she brushed her hand over his face and felt his breath pass over her palm.

"I'm too heavy for you." His voice was weak. "You can make it if you let go of me."

She secured her hold. She wasn't ready to let go of him. Not three years ago, nor since.

"No," she whispered, more to herself than to him. "I'm not letting you go."

The line tied around Sawyer went taut. She barely managed to hold on to him. Their bodies sloughed through the water as if on skis propelled by a motorboat.

Not a boat. The dogs. She raised her head toward where a light shone. And glimpsed the silhouette of a child.

Framed in the light streaming from inside the house, Max summoned the black Labs forward. "Come on, Blackie," he urged above the wind and rain. "You can do it. You can make it. Come on. Keep swimming. Come to Max."

Yard by yard, foot by foot, the dogs strained, weighted by their humans. But they were relentless. Persevering. Never stopping. Never giving up.

Her knees scraped against something hard and unyielding. The steps. She struggled to find her footing. A tidal surge sent them the rest of the way. And she found herself cast like driftwood hurtling across the remaining distance toward the doorway.

She yanked Sawyer through the doorframe. Max worked frantically at untying the rope before a receding wave could drag the dogs and Sawyer out toward the depths again. Flotsam streamed past what had once been the living room. And the water continued to rise.

With Blackie and Ajax free, Max helped her lug Sawyer toward the safety of the stairs. "Upstairs," Honey shouted. "I've got him." Paws scrabbling, the dogs raced toward the landing. Max scrambled after them.

Sawyer's arm slung around her shoulders, she pushed through the waist-high water. His feet dragging, Sawyer stumbled and fell against the newel post.

He righted himself and rung by rung pulled himself up the staircase. "I'm okay. Go to Max. I'll be right behind you."

"No." She glared at him. "I'm not leaving you. You go first."

"Of all the hardheaded, stubborn..." He gritted his teeth and muttered a few other phrases too low for her ears to catch.

Something oily and coiled slithered past her leg. Her eyes widened. She screamed.

Grabbing a floating umbrella from the overturned coat tree, Sawyer pinned the copperhead to the wall and smashed his head. She fought the bile rising in her throat.

Another triangular head broke the surface of the water lapping against the stairs. Two more followed. The hurricane had shifted loose a nest of vipers. She screamed again.

"Get upstairs," he yelled. "I've got this."

And this time, she didn't argue. She darted up the remaining stairs to the sounds of Sawyer beating back the sea-loosed serpents.

She charged onto the second floor to find Max leaning over the railing, cheering Sawyer on. "Smack 'em. Whack 'em."

"Max, get away from there." She prodded him once again toward Amelia and Braeden's room. Where she found the dogs curled under the bed.

"You're wet again," she clucked. "But you were so smart and brave." Peeling off Max's shirt, she toweled his carroty locks dry.

"So were you."

Honey glanced up to find Sawyer, breathing hard, leaning against the doorway. Blood trickled down the side of his head. His face pale, he swayed and caught hold of the doorframe.

"I don't like the look of that cut. You took quite a blow." She grasped his arm. "You could have a concussion."

"Hard head. You should know." He gave her a semblance of the former cocksure King of the Rodeo smile. "I'll be fine."

She tugged him toward her father's room. "You need to get out of those wet clothes. We need to get you warm before you go into shock."

He gave her a lopsided grin, curling her toes. "That sounds like the most promising thing I've heard in ages."

She propped him against the bureau. "You must be okay, cowboy, if you're able to flirt. Though I suspect it's so second nature, you'll be flirting from your deathbed, too."

"Only if you're standing bedside at the time." A small smile quirked one corner of his mouth. "What can I say? You inspire me."

She ignored him and pulled one of her father's shirts and a pair of jeans out of a drawer. "Here."

He shied away. "That belongs to your dad."

She arched a brow. "You will wear these or catch your death of pneumonia. Don't make me go all Amelia on you, Sawyer. You wouldn't like it."

He snagged the clothing from her arms. "You're right. I wouldn't. 'Cause I like you the way you are, Beatrice."

She rolled her eyes. "Now I know you're feeling better."

He shuffled his feet. "You saved my life out there."

"Just doing what anyone would've done. God and those dogs saved us both."

"But you saved me first. Long time ago, too." His eyes bored into hers. "In more ways than one."

She put a hand to her throat.

"And you know what they say when someone saves your life where I come from, Beatrice?"

"No. What do they say, Sawyer?" she whispered.

He gave her the old smile that used to send her knees a-knocking. Still did, apparently. She caught hold of the edge of the bureau.

"They say when a person saves your life, you belong to that person forever."

Forever? She swallowed. That's how long she suspected she'd be in love with this brash guardsman.

Sawyer leaned forward. She held her breath.

And the lights went out, plunging them into the darkness.

Chapter Nine

"Drink this. The coffee's hot."

Sawyer took the mug from Honey. His hand momentarily covered hers before she scooted away. Clad in Seth's red-checked flannel shirt and jeans, Sawyer's teeth chattered as he huddled around the kerosene lantern on the floor of the second-story common area at the top of the stairs.

Dry and his belly full of stale Long Johns, Max had recovered his energy. Baseball bat in hand, he and the dogs hunched over the top step, waiting for the next sea creature to invade their domain.

Sawyer flicked a glance at Honey. She'd not said much since the lights went out an hour ago. His heart lurched. Thrilled beyond measure to be this close to the woman he'd never stopped loving, yet he worried as the water crept up the stairs. The wind velocity had increased to an ear-shattering wail.

The nineteenth-century house, built to last against nature's fury, groaned. The walls and eaves vibrated. Any minute the house and its timbers could be torn apart, hurling them into the deep. Or as the flooding increased, they could climb higher to her third-story bedroom. But they could become trapped by the attic ceiling and drown.

"I wish I had an axe."

Her eyes darted to his.

"So, if worse comes to worst, I can chop a way onto the roof." Where perhaps they could hold on long enough for the storm to subside and rescue to come. Better to leave that part unvoiced.

But he didn't fool her. She'd always been able to see right into his head. And into his heart.

Those big, sunflower-brown eyes of hers widened. "The roof?" She glanced toward the ceiling and shuddered at the howling cacophony swirling outside the walls.

He frowned. Last thing he wanted was to scare her. He'd give his life if it meant protecting her from harm.

Rising, she disappeared into the flickering shadows cast by the lantern toward another bedroom. She returned clutching a quilt to her chest. Advancing, she draped the quilt around Sawyer. His breath caught.

The alluring essence of Honey Duer filled his senses. Her signature flowery fragrance clung to the quilt she tucked around his body.

Sawyer buried his nostrils into its folds and inhaled. Talk about crazy. He'd awoken one night from a dead sleep in his apartment in San Diego to this never-forgotten perfume. Convinced for a millisecond before reality returned, they'd found each other again. But just a dream. A hopeless dream.

Honey put a hand to the bandage she'd rigged over his temple. Her fingers drifted. For a second, her warm palm cupped his high cheekbones. He closed his eyes. If this was a dream, then he never wanted to awaken.

Sawyer's heart sank. He'd never stopped loving her. But he'd never be good enough for her, either. There would—could—never be a chance of a future with her.

His face chilled as she removed her hand. He opened his eyes to find her beside him, her back pressed against the interior wall. The safest place—if such a place existed for them—in the midst of the raging tumult of the storm.

Max tired of his vigil. He inched over to the pallet next to the lantern. Bracketed by his faithful canine companions, he closed his eyes and slept.

As suddenly as if switching off a faucet, the deafening banshee stopped. Sawyer's ears continued to ring for a moment. And it took him another second to recognize they'd entered at long last the eye of the storm. Total peace. Total calm.

Until the western wall of the hurricane swept over their oasis once more. Thirty minutes? He had at most that much time to assess their situation and maximize their chances of survival before the wind returned with a vengeance. He stirred.

She snared his shirtsleeve. "Where are you going?"

Though as tall as the older man, the jeans were snug on his frame. The shirt hung loose and untucked over a tan Henley, which also belonged to her father.

Sawyer inched up the wall. He shrugged out of the quilt. Grabbing the lantern, he gripped the cold glass doorknob of a guest room and pushed open the door.

Bunching the quilt in her arms, Honey stepped inside the room after him. "You're still shivering. Keep this around your body."

He strode to the window. "Stop fussing. I'm okay."

At the sight that met his eyes, he considered retracting that statement. In the dim light, nothing but water stretched as far as the eye could see. The dock had disappeared. The water lapped halfway up the pine trees dividing the main house from the cabin.

She quivered. "Oh, Sawyer. If it continues to rise, what will we do?"

Honey, born and bred on the storm-prone Shore, probably knew more than he about the dangers. "My granddad was a boy during the big one, Hazel, in '33. A wall of water overran their barrier island home."

She sighed. "The Duers and everyone else, including the life-saving station that predated Station Kiptohanock, abandoned the island for good. But no one alive at the time—" she gulped "—or at least those who lived to tell about it, ever forgot. Even here on the mainland, people were found clinging to life in the uppermost branches of trees. Babies ripped from their mother's arms, their little bodies never found. Boats shoved five miles ashore. Homes demolished and washed out to sea."

Honey trembled. "I've read about what happened to the island of Galveston, too, and those people trapped by the floodwaters in their homes at the turn of the twentieth century. We're going to die, aren't we?"

Before he remembered how much she hated him, he put his arms around her. And she didn't pull away. Instead, she leaned into him and rested her forehead against the hollow of his shoulder.

"This isn't Galveston. We're not going to die. I won't let anything happen to you and Max, I promise." He ground his teeth. "I know you don't believe in my promises. Rightly so. But no matter what I have to do, I'll make sure you're safe."

She nestled closer. "You have to be safe, too."

His safety didn't matter. He'd barely gotten off Shore three years ago before he realized that in saving Honey's future, he'd lost his own. For the first time since Braeden negotiated his reassignment to Kiptohanock, he breathed a prayer of gratitude. Perhaps God had brought him back for this—to save Honey's life.

Whatever God's purpose, he allowed himself to relish the feel of Honey in his arms. Something he'd never dared imagine would be his privilege ever again. Not after he'd cut her loose without an explanation for her own good. Saving her for Charlie Pruitt.

His heart knotted. In the end, saving her was the only thing that mattered. Then and now. He let go of her and stepped away.

"Let's see what we can scrounge up if we need to break out of our watery prison."

She sighed and her arms dropped to her sides. "A prison of our own making?"

"My making. My fault." He turned away lest she see the sudden welling of his eyes. "Charlie Pruitt's a lucky man..."

"What?"

Squaring his shoulders, he moved around her.

"Wait." She caught his arm. "Sawyer..."

His heart pounded at the touch of her hand. How he wanted to hold her. Forever. To never let her go. To show her how much he loved her.

But cool reason prevailed. What he really wished was that he'd been born someone else. Someone other than the son of a convict and drug-addicted mother. Anyone else. More deserving of a sweet, gentle woman like Honey Duer and her remarkable, faithful family.

He reluctantly, but firmly, twisted free. And ached inside at the confusion etched across her lovely oval face.

"Why won't you talk to me?"

Sawyer turned toward the hall. Call it pride or self-protection. Because if ever he explained who he really was, he couldn't bear her pity. "Best thing we can do is pray."

Honey gave him a mock salute. "Have been and will continue to do so, Petty Officer."

Sawyer slipped across the hall, past Max and his snoring Labs, to Seth's room. She dogged his heels. He set the lantern on top of the dresser.

"Here's hoping your dad has some tools squirreled away

inside the house. Life preservers are probably too much to hope for." He wrested open the closet door. "I thought you were mad at God."

"I'm working on that. I'm mainly mad at you."

He laughed and rummaged through Seth's closet. "Good to know, Beatrice."

She huffed. Which made him laugh again.

"I'm glad to hear you and God are communicating."

She leaned against the bedpost. "Why is it whenever you're around, I always seem to find myself in a storm? And then one way or the other, you or it drive me to my knees."

He grinned.

She steeled herself against the all too familiar buckling of her knees. His smile ought to be licensed. And that cocky Coastie probably knew it.

"Glad I could be of service. Always Ready is our motto. 'Cause in the Guard, we—"

"Live to serve." She waved her hand. "I know, I know. So you've told me. I just want us to live through this never-ending day."

He disappeared into the confines of her father's closet. Sawyer reemerged, triumph glowing in his blue eyes, a fire ladder in his hands. "If worse comes to worst—"

"Every time you say that," she moaned. "It does."

His lips quirked. "I meant we'll make our own lifeboat out of anything floatable. Break a window and crawl out."

She wrapped her arms around the quilt, clutching it to her chest. "Get into the water again?"

His eyebrows rose. "What happened to my brave Shore queen now?" His eyes glinted with mischief.

"She did her best and then decided she'd rather go shopping."

"Her best saved my life." He gestured toward the common area. "And only you could turn a natural disaster into something cozy."

"I'm not sure that's a compliment."

"I'm sure enough for both of us." He broadened his shoulders. "And might I also say that you glow in the lantern light? Always the most beautiful woman I've ever known."

Something released in her heart and soared free. She'd not understood until this moment how his walking away had shattered her confidence. "Then why did you…?"

Clenching his jaw and carrying the rope ladder, he walked out of the room, leaving her question unanswered. But she found him waiting for her at the end of the narrow hallway. At the door to the walkup attic she'd converted into her own special place.

If he wouldn't answer her questions about the past, perhaps he'd open up about more recent events.

She held the lantern to his face. "Where did you get the scar on your jaw?"

He reddened. "A mission gone wrong."

"San Diego?"

"No. After that." He stared at her. "You knew I was in San Diego? Were you keeping track?"

Her turn to blush. "I wasn't keeping track." So not true. "I—I was making sure we kept our distance."

Sawyer motioned toward the attic stairs. "Can we check out the condition of the roof?"

Honey ushered him forward. "Be my guest."

Sawyer stepped through with a strange look in his eyes as if *he* didn't quite trust *her*. Holding the light aloft, she brushed past him on the stairs and blazed the trail toward what had always been her refuge from every storm life threw her way. Her mom's death, her dad's depression, Lindi's death and Max's cancer. And somehow most devastating of all, Sawyer's abandonment.

He moved beyond the quilt-covered sleigh bed to the window.

"So what happened to your face?"

He didn't turn around. "Adds so much to my features, don't you think? Makes me look dangerous and more ruggedly handsome."

"You're dangerous, all right." Dangerous to every red-blooded American female heart. Or at least, dangerous to hers.

"And handsome...?"

She sniffed. "Vain much, Kole?"

He laughed. As she'd meant him to. The tension in his shoulders eased a notch. She fought a desperate urge to wrap her arms around him.

She'd missed this easiness with him. An almost instinctive familiarity she'd never found with any other man. The lighthearted banter and the surprisingly tender, heartfelt talks of that long ago spring had made Sawyer Kole possibly the best friend she'd ever had.

"The scar?" she prompted in an urgent need to take her mind off the past and the gaping uncertainty of their present.

He deposited the rope on the window seat. "If you must know, maritime law enforcement with a Central American task force in the Caribbean. Drug interdiction. Boat chase ended with my team boarding a fast boat. My chin," he adjusted his jaw with his hand. "Caught the sharp end of a knife."

She gasped and laced her fingers through his. "You need to be more careful, Sawyer."

"Tell that to the cornered drug lord." He blew out a slow breath. "But no worries, he's cooling his heels in a Mexican prison as we speak. And I'm doing okay." He ran his thumb over her hand. "Actually today, I'm feeling better than okay."

"Says the Coastie trapped in a hurricane with a little boy, two dogs and an innkeeper whose only skills are more decorative than essential."

He let go of her hand and grasped both of her shoulders. "Someone as pretty as you doesn't have to be anything other than what she already is. And for your information, Beatrice, your presence is essential to everyone who loves you." A pulse pounded in the hollow of his throat.

Sawyer dropped his hands and moved away. "I'm glad you were able to save the family portrait." He gazed at the framed photo she'd deposited earlier for safekeeping on her bed. "Your sister Caroline looks the most like your mom. Whatever happened to Caroline?"

Honey shrugged. "After Mom died, Caroline returned to college off-Shore and never came back. We get Christmas cards. But nothing else. Dad can't even bear to say her name. So none of us bring her up."

She traced the outline of her mother's face in the portrait with her eye. "This house..." Her voice broke. "Was all I had left of Mom. And Caroline. The last place we were together as a family. I don't understand how someone walks away from everyone who loves them and never looks back."

He hooked Honey about the waist, surprising her into a hug.

"Perhaps Caroline believed she had to leave. Like she had no other choice. Maybe the best choice for the people who loved her." Both arms around her torso, he pressed Honey's spine against his chest.

"How could that kind of loss be best for her or those who loved her so much? How could you—?"

"We're going to get out of here." His mouth grazed the top of her head. "And you'll always have your home if I have to personally reframe and nail this house together again myself."

She angled. Placing her palm against his shirt, she felt the drumbeat of his heart through the fabric. "Why would you do that for me, Sawyer? Why, if you stopped caring for me that way?"

With a sudden crescendo, the wind picked up speed. Torrents of rain slashed against the glass panes. Something thudded against the roof overhead. She jerked.

"Because I never stopped…" He bit his lip so hard dots of blood appeared.

Leaning closer, she ran her finger across his bottom lip and wiped away the smear of blood. "You never stopped what, Sawyer?"

His eyes locked onto hers. "I—"

"Aunt Honey? Where are you? Sawyer?" Max's panicked cries sounded below.

Releasing her, Sawyer jerked toward the stairs.

The moment passed and she hurried after him to comfort her nephew who'd awoken frightened by the renewed intensity of the storm.

In truth, she grimaced as she enfolded Max in her arms, her moment and Sawyer's had passed a long time ago. Three years ago. On a moonlit beach outside Ocean City.

Chapter Ten

Hours later, Honey awoke to utter silence. A silence all the more eerie in contrast with the nightlong banshee of the wind. Stiff, she shifted, careful not to wake Max.

The air lay heavy and moist on her skin. But they were alive. They'd survived, and the hurricane had blown itself out to sea.

A yawning pit opened in her stomach. Her gaze ping-ponged. She bolted upright.

"Sawyer?" she yelled. Max stirred in her arms. She disentangled herself from his arms entwined around her neck.

"Mimi?" he murmured, his eyes still closed. "I want Mimi."

Panic clawed at her heart. "Sawyer? Answer me. Where are you?" Laying Max aside, she scrabbled to her feet.

"It's okay, Beatrice," Sawyer called from below the landing. "I'm down here."

Max sat up and stretched. "Is it over? I'm hungry."

She hurried toward the stairs. Her pulse leaped at the sight of the bandaged Coastie leaning against the stairwell. Light from the open door and broken windows dappled the contours of his face.

"The water's already receded. Like somebody pulled

the stopper on a bathtub." He dropped his eyes. "But it's a real mess. I'm sorry."

She gulped. "I may blame you for a lot, Sawyer Kole. But I'm pretty sure Hurricane Zelda was beyond your control."

He held out his hand. "Just remember, everything can be fixed. The important thing is we're alive."

She slid her hand in his and allowed him to help her step over the debris cluttering the staircase. She made her way to what had once been the first floor of seven generations of Duers.

Her feet encased in muck, she gasped, unprepared for the complete devastation. She covered her mouth and nose with her hand. The brackish stench overwhelmed her senses.

All the money she'd spent on the remodel gone to waste. Her eyes welled. The waterline, like the dirty ring on a bathtub, etched the four walls.

She closed her eyes, unable to cope with the total destruction of her childhood home and the complete demolition of her greatest dream. The ground floor—kitchen, dining room, living room and stairs—was a total loss. The home equity loan she'd taken out and was still repaying for naught. She sagged, the spiraling debt dragging her downward as if she were caught in an oceanic vortex.

He hugged her close. "It's going to be okay. I told you. All of this is fixable."

She shook her head. "I'm without resources and out of business for the duration."

"You're not without resources. You've got friends and neighbors—"

"Whose homes and businesses are probably as destroyed as mine."

"And you've got me."

She stepped out of the circle of his arms. "Since when have I ever had you?"

He folded his arms over his chest. "Glad to see you haven't lost that fighting Duer spirit."

She waved her arm. "Yeah, probably the only thing I've got left now."

"Bitterness doesn't become you, Beatrice." Mouth twisting, he turned toward the gaping front entrance. "God will make a way."

Shame darkened her cheeks. His all too apparent disappointment in her stung. Her mouth quivered.

"Don't remember you and God being so buddy-buddy when you courted me up and down the Delmarva three years ago, Kole." Her chest heaved. "I also don't believe you're standing on any moral high ground yourself after the way you dumped me."

Sawyer pivoted so suddenly, she took an involuntary step backward, her Wellingtons squelching in the mud.

In two sloshing strides, he was at her side, grasping her elbows. "You don't know anything about my relationship with God. And you're right. Three years ago, God and I weren't on speaking terms. But a lot has changed. Something you'd already know about if you weren't so determined to make me the culminating scapegoat for every bad thing that's ever happened in your life.

His face hardened. "Truth is, we were no good to each other then. Maybe God had a higher purpose in separating us than either you or I could imagine at the time."

"Don't you dare preach to me about God. What kind of higher purpose? What kind of way did God make when my mother lay dying of ovarian cancer?" Honey smacked her fist into his chest. He staggered.

"When Daddy fell into a decade-long depression and his heart almost gave out?" She shoved Sawyer. "When Lindi died with Max in her arms—"

"Aunt Honey..." A small voice wobbled from above. "Why are you yelling at Sawyer? Why are you being mean again?"

The black Labs' noses poked through the banister. Their tongues lolled, hassling.

Max's face looked small and scared as he hung over the railing. "Mimi says stuff happens not 'cause God doesn't love us, but 'cause that's the way it is down here. 'Cause this isn't our final home."

Honey grabbed the newel post for support. Was that the problem? She'd made this house her god? Like once, three years ago, she'd put Sawyer before God and her family?

Max jutted his jaw. "When my birth mom died, Mimi became my forever mom. And God made a way for Braeden to be my dad, too."

She squeezed her eyes shut. The anger and bitterness were a cancer that had squeezed out everything good and right in her life. Max's childlike faith smote her conscience.

"I love Sawyer, Aunt Honey. I thought you did, too."

She opened her eyes. That was the problem. She couldn't deny the truth any longer. Only someone she'd loved that deeply had the power to wound her so deeply. Clamping her lips together, she didn't trust herself to speak. Afraid she'd fall to pieces.

"Thank you for your vote of confidence, buddy." Sawyer moved away from Honey, his eyes hooded. "I love you, too."

She hardened her heart. Words Sawyer Kole had never spoken to her. He'd used her that spring. She'd been just another diversion, a babe in every port. "What makes you think, Coastie, we're any good to each other now?"

He flinched as if she'd physically struck him. His eyes dulled. His face resumed the stoic expression he wore of late.

She wanted to weep. Hurting him as he'd hurt her

somehow didn't provide the satisfaction she'd imagined. "Sawy—"

"Ahoy in the house!" Braeden's voice bellowed from outside.

Max took the stairs two at a time, vaulting over the debris toward the ground floor. "Dad? It's me, Max. I'm here."

Braeden along with an EMT from Riverside clambered up what remained of the porch.

"Max!" The relief on Braeden's face as he spotted his son nearly broke Honey. Braeden opened his arms wide as Max crossed the distance between them and jumped into his embrace. Braeden buried his dark, short-cropped Coastie head into Max's scrawny neck.

The child trembled with repressed sobs. "I knew you'd come. I knew you'd find me."

Braeden's shoulder blades twitched. He stroked Max's back as if not just reassuring the little boy. Braeden's chocolate-brown eyes lifted, scanning the destruction. Sizing up the tension and gulf between Sawyer and Honey with one glance. "Everybody okay, here?"

"Sawyer saved my life, Dad. Blackie and Ajax, too."

Braeden blinked away the moisture in his eyes. "Seems I continue to be in your debt, Petty Officer. Now you've gone and saved my son. How can Amelia and I ever thank you?"

Sawyer went into regulation stance, arms rigid at his sides. "Just doing my duty, Chief. And it was your sister-in-law who saved me actually."

His duty? Is that what last night had been?

Honey slumped against the soggy wall. "We saved each other. How is Amelia?"

Braeden held Max close. "Resting at the hospital with your dad. Baby Scott decided the middle of a hurricane was not the best time to make an appearance after all."

Sawyer raked a hand over his face. “Smart kid.”

Braeden nodded. “Let’s get you all out of here.”

She stiffened.

“For now, Honey.” Braeden motioned toward a waiting four wheel drive truck. “Everyone’s meeting at the church to count heads. Giving thanks to God so far no one appears to be unaccounted for. Kiptohanock needs time to regroup and plan the recovery. God will be our strength.”

She cut her eyes at Sawyer. He avoided her gaze and broad-shouldered his way out the door, leaving her to follow. Or not.

That was the trouble, she reflected. God might be Sawyer’s strength—a mind-boggling notion considering the Coastie she’d known three years ago. As for her? She’d lost that kind of strength somewhere along the way.

Or worse yet? Perhaps she’d never possessed that sort of strength in the first place.

Chapter Eleven

It bothered Sawyer that Kiptohanock's church steeple tilted. No longer an upright beacon of hope to mariners and townsfolk. But Kiptohanock hadn't fared as poorly as the lodge. Once the waters receded, there appeared to be minimal damage to the village. Most fishing vessels, Seth and Braeden's boats included, were dry-docked farther inland and out of harm's way.

Running on a generator, the diner became a gathering spot for residents to grab a cup of coffee and a hot meal until electricity could be restored Shore-wide. Practically dead on his feet, Sawyer felt compelled to return immediately to duty watch.

The station hummed with activity. The crew, alongside county law enforcement and volunteer fire departments, performed countless missions in the surrounding area to rescue people trapped inside their homes. But as the afternoon of the first day after Zelda drew to a close, things had slowed enough for Braeden to send Sawyer off duty.

Instead, he gathered outside the church with the other Kiptohanock citizens at Reverend Parks's request. To give thanks that no lives were lost in the storm. To rejoice that barring the ripped-off roof shingles and Pisa-like steeple, the church had emerged intact.

Sawyer hung at the back of the crowd. He kept his distance from Honey and her dad near the steps of the church. She—according to Braeden—had spent the day in a cafe booth on the phone with an insurance rep. Reverend Parks moved in front of the double oak doors at the top of the steps.

"What're we going to do, Reverend?" A fiftysomething matron Sawyer recognized as the owner of the local outfitter shop. "I was counting on revenue from Harbor Fest this year."

Other heads—gray, brown, blond and red—nodded.

"Brings the tourists in by the droves." One of Seth's ROMEO compatriots, shrugged. "Without them, many of us are going to find ourselves unable to survive the long stretch of winter. Financially speaking."

Reverend Parks lifted his hand, and the buzz of conversation on the muddy front lawn of the church faded. "Friends, I realize the situation looks dire. I know this is the worst possible time to find ourselves in this position. But we can't lose heart. When circumstances look the darkest that is when our God shines the brightest. Perhaps all is not lost."

"You imagine we should still hold Harbor Fest?" The postmistress grumbled. "Look around, Reverend. Our town is a mess."

Seth stroked his mustache with his finger. "God hasn't let any of us down yet, and He's not about to start now. Kiptohanock will rally. We'll help each other. It's the Shore way."

Reverend Parks nodded. "We can't lose our hope, friends. Not now. This could be Kiptohanock's finest hour if we open our hearts and give God room to work in our lives and community."

Sawyer raised his hand. As XPO, he'd been appointed as the station's personal representative to the village.

Reverend Parks swung his way at the motion of his hand. "I know I speak for everyone here when I voice my deepest appreciation for what the United States Coast Guard did during the storm, Petty Officer."

Sawyer reddened. That wasn't why guardsmen did what they did, although appreciation was nice. But he didn't want to appear to be fishing for compliments. "I'm not a resident of Kiptohanock, but the station's been discussing what could be done for this town we've come to love and call home. At least, our temporary home."

Honey swiveled and scowled at him.

Sawyer thought it best to ignore her before he lost his train of thought. More of an adrenaline junkie, he was best suited to action. Public speaking ranked low on his list of all-time favorite jobs.

He took a breath. "We've pledged our personal funds and worked out a rotation of volunteers during off duty hours to reroof the sanctuary."

There were murmurs of approval.

Sawyer forged ahead through the difficult part of what he intended to say. Somehow to convey what he and the other guardsmen felt for the town and its citizens.

"The steeple—" He cleared his throat past his unaccustomed emotion. "It stands watch like a holy sentinel, not only over the inhabitants of coastal Kiptohanock, but also over the Coast Guardsmen in its midst. And so we'd also like to assist in restoring the steeple."

Claps and cheers broke out. Honey crossed her arms over her chest and bit her lip.

Reverend Parks raised his arms shoulder level. "Petty Officer, I'm overwhelmed and humbled by the Guard's generous offer. See, brothers and sisters. I told you. God has not abandoned us."

Sawyer winced at the reverend's choice of words.

"Let us bow our heads," the reverend called, "and give

thanks to the One who kept us anchored throughout a long, terrible night and brought us once more into the light of day."

Seth and the other ROMEOs removed their ball caps. Sawyer likewise removed his headgear and went into an at-ease position, his feet splayed to his hips.

"We praise You, O God," Reverend Parks intoned. "That You have gathered us here again today out of the wind and the rain and the storms of life."

Sawyer added his silent thanks to God.

"Grant us the courage to move forward despite the devastation around us. Help us to love our neighbor, in their hour of greatest need, more than we love ourselves."

Sawyer had made another decision, as well. Which would infuriate Honey. But it was a promise he couldn't walk away from, no matter how much his heart told him to run again before it was too late. It was the only decision he could make and still live with himself.

"Most of all, we pray to never lose sight of our ultimate hope in You." Reverend Parks clasped his hands. "Amen."

"Amen," the residents of Kiptohanock chorused.

Sawyer exhaled. During the storm last night, he'd begun to hope. He stuffed his hands in his pockets. Hope for what? How stupid could he get?

In the light of day, his optimism dimmed. There were no second chances for someone like him. He'd known that since he was a boy. And if Honey couldn't or wouldn't forgive him, why should God?

All the peace and strength he'd experienced since San Diego faded. Had he been fooling himself about his new relationship with God? What would God, much less Honey, want with a messed-up sinner like him anyway?

Sawyer edged farther back. Always on the outside looking in—story of his life. His truck overturned by the floodwaters was a total loss. Maybe he could get Reaves to give him a ride to his rented quarters at Pauline Crockett's farm where he lived.

He hoped—prayed if God listened to broken people like him—Miss Pauline, farther inland and on higher ground closer to Onley, had fared better. Best to slip away before— A hand clamped on his shoulder halted Sawyer in place.

Seth Duer's blue-green eyes narrowed. "Going somewhere, son?"

"Uh..." He'd faced modern-day pirates and drug lords, but Seth Duer was scarier.

Seth let loose of Sawyer to adjust the Nandua Warriors ball cap. "I can never thank you enough for being there for my baby girl and Max."

"Just doing my job, sir."

Seth cut his eyes at him. "I don't for a moment doubt you're a poster child for the Guard. But I also suspect duty has very little to do with anything between you and that daughter of mine."

"I'm no one's poster child." Sawyer folded his arms. "More like a foster child."

"And I think you underestimate yourself, though you do a great job covering your insecurity with that rodeo bravado. Anyway, I have a favor to ask of you."

He cocked an eyebrow at the older man.

"Friend of mine owns a spread farther up the neck. Stables and horses, right up your alley."

He wasn't sure where Honey's dad was going with this. "Yessir..."

"Tree landed on his car with him inside. Bad break. Both legs. He's going to be out of commission for a while. I know you and Braeden had this deal about transferring out this week, but wondered if you'd reconsider and see to the care and feeding of his animals while he's in rehab."

"I made Hon—I mean Beatrice—a promise during the

storm last night." He braced for Seth's hostility. "I've already spoken to Braeden about delaying my departure. I'd like to help restore the ground floor of the lodge. Get the Duers back in business as soon as possible. That is," he darted his eyes at Seth. "If you have no objection."

"You'll get no objection from me. It's a generous offer. We'd be foolish to refuse. We're gonna need every bit of manpower we can find if we hope to be up and running by Harbor Fest."

"Don't know that Beatrice will agree."

Seth fingered his jaw. "You let me handle Honey. Only one question."

"What's that, sir?"

"You still love my daughter, don't you?"

Sawyer worked to retain control of his mouth. He gave Seth a curt nod. "I do. But I'm not sure a relationship with me would be in her best interests." He hung his head.

"No buts about it, son." Seth grimaced. "I'll take you out to Keller's farm. You and I are long overdue for another little chat."

Crossing the parking lot, Sawyer climbed into the Silverado, which had escaped the storm's destruction. With downed trees and power lines, Honey's dad turned off Seaside Road and took a circuitous route.

Finally, Seth veered off the main traffic artery and followed a dirt driveway curving into the trees. They emerged into broad, open pastureland. Sawyer noted the Dutch-roofed, red-painted stable behind a two-story Victorian on a hilly rise.

He rolled down the window and took a deep cleansing breath. Hay and horse were his first loves before he'd taken off for the sea life of a Coastie.

Seth's lips curved. "I knew I was right in bringing you here if that's the reaction this smelly old farm gives you."

"Not smelly, Mr. Duer." His brow furrowed. "The best

of both worlds, I figure." He nudged his head to the thin sliver of blue beyond the house. "A sea breeze, too."

The older man grinned, the wrinkles caused by a lifetime of deep sea fishing rearranged themselves. "Keller's needed help with this place for half a decade. He's too stubborn to admit it's too much for him. The storm's sort of forced the issue of putting the farm on the market. I told him I had the perfect caretaker in the meantime. A bona fide cowboy."

"Me?" Sawyer scanned the rustic views. "It's a grand place. A little run down. But with some spit and polish, it'd be perfect for someone who loves horses."

Seth gave a satisfied sigh. "I knew you were the right man to catch the vision of what this place used to be.

"Could be again," Sawyer corrected. "Think a rich come-here will buy it?

Seth snorted. "Probably. Who else has that kind of money 'sides them?"

"I hear you, sir." He laughed. "Me and you work for a living."

Honey's dad eyed him. "Me and you got more in common than you think, young man."

Sawyer shifted. "I don't know what you mean."

"That's 'cause what I'm about to tell you I ain't never told another human being. 'Cept my Marian, God rest her soul."

"Sir, I don't know if you should—"

"My father, Kole, was what Grandmother Duer euphemistically called a ne'er do well."

Sawyer dropped his eyes.

"What the state of Virginia called a convicted criminal." Seth pursed his lips. "He died incarcerated in the state penitentiary when I was fourteen after he stabbed a man to death over a woman in Norfolk."

Sawyer knotted his hands together.

"Braeden told me how you're afeared you inherited a criminal gene from your father. That's nothing but a load of fish guts, son."

Sawyer inhaled sharply.

"Braeden also told me how you've got some mistaken notion you were saving Honey from yourself by walking away. How you believe the lies that sorry son of a biscuit eater told you. That you're no good and you don't deserve anything good in your life."

Seth Duer jutted his jaw. "And I'm here to tell you that's a lie. You're a rescuer, son. Not a destroyer. And I'm living proof you don't have to be what my brilliant daughter Caroline used to call a self-fulfilling prophecy."

The older man glanced away, his face pinched. "Too smart for her own good, my Caroline." He sighed. "But that's a story for another day."

"You don't understand, sir." Sawyer half turned in the seat. "My father said my mother only got addicted to heroin after I was born. That I ruined her. That because of me…"

Sawyer gripped the armrest. "He said… She left, died on the street, because of me."

"And you gonna believe anything that man told you?" Seth huffed. "He beat you, didn't he, Sawyer? When you were a boy?"

The shame he'd known as a child crept up his neck. "I—I deserved it. I ruined his life, too, when he had to marry my mother."

Honey's father caught his arm. "You didn't deserve any of that. No child does. She should have never left you. Not with him. But I'd guess she left to get away from *him*. Not *you*. 'Cause if he was beating on you, he started first on her."

A memory Sawyer hadn't recalled in a dozen years flew to the forefront of his mind. Of his mother sitting on the floor of the flophouse they called home in Tulsa. Nursing a welt to her cheek. Sobbing.

His stomach roiled. "All the more reason, sir… I'm not good enough for Honey or your family. Suppose I became like him or my mother?"

Sadness coated Seth Duer's features. "Same thing I told Marian Savage. She loved me anyway." Moisture dampened his eyes. "God, too. She told me that because of Him in me, I didn't have to become my father."

The waterman blew out a breath. "Nor my mother, either. Although I've been less successful…" His mouth tightened. "Again, a story for another day."

Honey's dad scrubbed his hand over his face as if trying to dislodge bad memories. "My point, son, is that none of us deserve anything but for the grace and mercy of God. You know what grace is? Or mercy?"

Sawyer shook his head, his throat thick. He'd failed everyone who ever loved him.

"Grace is getting something we don't deserve." Seth's eyes bored into his. "Like with Jesus, a second chance and forgiveness."

Sawyer fisted his hands.

"And mercy? Mercy is not getting what we so richly deserve. What our sins deserve. Do you hear me, son?"

Sawyer cast his eyes to the floorboard. "I can't really fathom a God—anybody—who could love somebody as broken as me."

Honey's father smiled. "As broken as all of us. Who can truly grasp that sort of love?"

"That's God's kind of love. Not human love. I hurt Honey and no matter how much I wish I could have a do-over, there are consequences." Sawyer raked his hand over his head, sending his headgear akilter. "She'll never trust me again. Never allow me a second chance at her heart."

Sawyer blinked rapidly. "Crazy to think a Martha

Stewart wannabe would ever want anything to do with a washed-up cowboy like me."

Honey's father patted his arm. "I happen to know you set that girl of mine's heart aquiver every time you walk in the room. That—not you—is what makes her so furious. With herself. God's given you a second chance, not only with Him but with Honey, too. A second chance to prove to her your feelings are real and true."

If only Sawyer believed he stood a chance at winning back her respect and love.

Honey's father flung open the door. "Way I see it, you've got about two months before Harbor Fest to convince my daughter of your trustworthiness. But first? Let me introduce you to a few horses."

Seth's faith in him strengthened Sawyer's burgeoning resolve. For the first time, hope took root in his heart. Warring against his feelings of inadequacy.

Whatever it took, whatever he had to do—Sawyer refused to give up on the best thing outside of God he'd ever known.

If Beatrice Elizabeth Duer believed she could get rid of him so easily, she had another think coming.

Chapter Twelve

It was over. Honey's dream ruined. Her dream of a forever home swept out to sea with the hurricane.

She felt as if she'd lost her mother all over again. The ground floor was a total wreck. Like her life. Her hard work and the money she'd borrowed down the drain. She ached with a certainty that once FEMA inspected the lodge, the engineer would declare the structure unsound and that her family home would be torn down.

Although the hurricane had downgraded to Category 2 by the time it hit the peninsula, the Duers weren't the only ones affected by the destruction of the storm. Eastern Shore–tough, the Kiptohanockians rallied. Twenty families had been displaced by the floodwaters. But on the Eastern Shore, neighbors helped neighbors.

Surveying the devastation the day after, sadness engulfed Honey. Overwhelmed her as surely as the waves had swallowed the first floor of the lodge on which she'd pinned her hopes. She'd never felt so alone in her life.

In the immediate aftermath of the storm, with the Bay Bridge damaged, the only access onto the peninsula came from Maryland to the north. The governor of Virginia declared a state of emergency, clearing the way for FEMA to speed the process of recovery. The National Guard arrived to clear road debris. A long line of utility trucks from as far away as New Jersey made the journey south to restore electricity and phone service.

Recovery, like Honey's dream, would be a slow process. The village settled into a long haul of rebuilding.

Making a personal visit to the Delmarva Peninsula by helicopter from Richmond that first day, the governor promised he'd do everything in his power to help the locals file their insurance claims for reimbursement. But residents knew only those with deep pockets could afford to begin the rebuilding process without the insurance checks.

Some didn't even have flood coverage. She'd been round and round with their adjustor arguing over whether the damage to the inn resulted from the hurricane winds or the tidal surge which followed. Either way, the dickering could take weeks if not months. Time she didn't have if she wanted the inn back up and running. If that was even a possibility.

The day after the storm, a structural engineer declared the inn sound, but unlivable, until the downstairs had been restored. Sawyer relinquished the second floor efficiency he rented at Pauline Crockett's farmhouse and insisted the Duer family take up temporary residence.

She'd seen little of Sawyer. Out of sight, out of mind. Only the first part of that equation holding true. Where he spent his nights, she hadn't a clue. Their so-called date had been put on indefinite hold. Which was exactly the way she preferred things, she tried to convince herself.

Then out of the blue on Day Three post-Zelda, the Eastern Shore Bank in Onancock called to say they'd received money for the Duer account. She couldn't believe the insurance had settled so fast.

"God is good," her dad reminded her.

So they began making plans for the renovation. But the Duers, like their neighbors, would have to get in line for a reputable contractor to tackle the remodel. Former high school boyfriend and now sheriff's deputy, Charlie Pruitt, arrested a dozen scam artist contractors who arrived in droves to feed on the misery of beleaguered homeowners.

Seventy-two hours after the storm, Honey parked her father's truck at the muddy remnants of the circle drive to give her old home a thorough assessment and compile a punch list of jobs to be completed.

"A Honey Do-er list," her father joked.

Portions of the wraparound porch had been ripped away by the tide. It would be one of the first items on the check-list so workers could access the interior.

Careful to test each splintered board, she climbed to the open entrance. Once over the threshold, the wreckage took her breath. She wrinkled her nose at the pungent smells of mold and mildew, which in the humid air left by the storm, flourished unchecked.

Her eyes cut to the destroyed hand-carved mantel. No amount of twenty-first-century know-how could fix that. She moaned, the sound echoing off the twelve-foot ceiling.

"Why, God?" Honey stalked over to the fireplace. "Why did you allow this to happen?"

She pounded her fist on the dented and mangled mantelpiece. "Why did you take my mother and Lindi?" She rested her forehead against the battered wood. "Why does everyone always leave me?"

Behind Honey, a plank creaked. "Like me, you mean?"

She whirled, her heart thundering.

It was Sawyer, in a grubby baseball shirt, jeans and tool belt slung around his narrow waist who filled the gaping entrance. In his hand, he clutched a bunch of the yellow daisies with brown centers, which grew wild along Shore ditch banks in autumn.

She put a hand to her mouth. How much of that embarrassing stroll through her soul's darkest corners had he overheard? She gestured at the flowers. “Where’d you find those?”

A soft smile curved his lips. Lips that once kissed hers. On a beach in the moonlight—she snatched her thoughts away from that precipice.

He strode forward in his work boots. “These somehow managed to survive the salt water and wind. They’ve also become my favorite flower in the past few years.”

“Why’s that?”

He laid them lengthwise across the gouged surface of the mantel. “Because they remind me of you. Brown-eyed Susans, we call ’em in Oklahoma. With your blond hair and brown eyes, that’s what my foster mother would’ve called you, too.” He ducked his head.

Foster mother? Sawyer grew up in a foster home? She blinked. Why hadn’t she known that about him? Something so fundamental…

That long ago spring they’d talked of many things. Okay—mainly she talked. Of her frustrations with Amelia’s demands she return off-Shore to finish a college degree Honey didn’t want. Of her father babying her. Of the family home and vacation destination she wanted to create.

Her. Her. Her.

Only now, she realized how self-absorbed she’d been—still was, to hear her dad tell it. Sawyer had listened. Drawing out of Honey her hopes and dreams and fears. Of himself, he’d shared little.

Cracking funny jokes about his adventures at Basic. Humorous anecdotes about the inadvertent mayhem caused by clueless recreational boaters he encountered at Kiptohanock.

She’d thought she knew the essential things about Sawyer. That he loved horses and the sea. The color blue and long walks on the beach under the stars. She’d believed him sweet, funny and most of all, completely trustworthy and sincere.

Watching him interact with his Coastie colleagues, she recognized early he put on a front for the world. She'd been too immature to question why he'd felt the need to do so. Instead, she'd been flattered that to her—of all the people in the world—he'd given glimpses of his heart and the real Sawyer Kole underneath the Coastie cowboy bravado.

At least that's what she believed until he'd abandoned her on a beach in Ocean City. Was there more to the story—Sawyer's story—than what she imagined she knew? In hindsight, there were a lot of questions she should've asked him then.

"Why did you bring them here?" She cleared her throat.

Avoiding her eyes, he busied himself unloading his tools. "Your dad and Braeden told me they finished dragging everything out of the first floor yesterday. They plan to begin demolition this weekend on Braeden's off days. But with my shift over, I figured I'd give them a head start this afternoon."

"You didn't answer my question."

He removed a crowbar from a tool chest. "Amelia said you were dropping by tomorrow." He coughed. "I brought them for you. I knew seeing the place this way would gut you."

She stared at him. A muscle jerked in his throat. His gaze swung to hers and back to the floorboards.

"Thank you, Sawyer," she whispered. "That was very thoughtful of you."

His mouth tightened. He strode with purpose toward the wall against which once the sofa had rested. "You probably should leave so you don't have to see this." He knelt and inserted the pry bar between the wall and the baseboard.

"Wait." She hurried over, catching his arm. "What are you doing?"

"Starting with the baseboards and trim, I've got to rip out the dry wall. Everything down to the studs, joists and wiring. Which will need to be rewired by a professional. But otherwise, I promised you I'd give you back your home, Beatrice, and that's exactly what I intend to do."

He nudged his chin toward the open door. "Best be on your way."

She planted her hand on her hip. "Are you trying to get rid of me? I'll have you know I didn't intend to just 'drop by.' I intend, despite what you think of my girly-girl self, to be completely involved in restoring my home to its full beauty."

Rising, his eyes glinted. "Nothing wrong with your girly-girl self, I keep telling you, Beatrice." He broadened his shoulders. "I'm right glad you're a girl."

Sawyer grinned. "And beautiful, too. If you're determined to help, while I'm ripping out the baseboards you can locate and mark the screws and nails with this stud finder."

He reached over to a toolbox beside the sawhorse and extracted a palm-size device. Aiming it at a section of the wall, he swept the machine upward and sideways. He stopped at the sound of a ping.

Extracting a pencil from his pocket, he marked the spot. "Easy. See?" He handed the device to her.

Giving him a look, she scanned the beam over the next section and was rewarded with additional beeps. After marking the studs, she smiled at him over her shoulder. "A stud finder, you say?"

Eyes narrowing at her tone, he rocked on his heels and folded his arms across his chest. "Yeah… So?"

She ran the beam from his head to his steel-plated work boots. "Hate to disillusion you, but as I suspected, no studs here."

His eyebrows arched and those dimples she'd loved widened, bracketing his mouth. He lunged. "Give me that thing."

She danced away, raising the gadget high above her head, dodging out of his reach.

"Bee-ahh-triss..."

Laughing, she turned on her heel and darted for the stairs.

Giving chase, his arm caught her around the waist. Her back pressed against his chest, they wrestled for the stud finder. They stumbled into the railing.

"Are all cowboys as annoying as you, Sawyer?"

"Are all the Duer girls as aggravating as you, Beatrice?" he grunted. "Give it up, Girly-Girl."

Encircled by his arms and trapped against the staircase, she cocked her head. "I'll surrender the stud finder..." She moistened her lips. "For a kiss."

With a quick, indrawn breath, he let go of her. "I thought you hated me."

She clutched the device to her chest. "Maybe, like you said, it's time to revisit this thing between us. Probably wasn't as great or big a thing as we imagined. Get it out of our systems once and for all and finally move on."

He took a step backward, and she immediately missed his warmth. "Let me get this straight. You want me to kiss you?"

She laid the stud finder between the rungs on the stair step. "I do."

Honey lifted her chin and moved closer. "For old time's sake. Give it your best shot, Kole." She fondled the pearl stud on her earlobe.

A skittish look in his eyes, he knotted his hands against the sides of the jeans that fit him oh so right. But he didn't move. Made no attempt to come near or to touch her. He gazed at her, two...three...five seconds.

Doubt assailed her. What had gotten into her? Suppose he didn't want to…?

His Adam's apple bobbed in his throat and in a sudden move, he took hold of her forearms. He lowered his head. Her lips parted, and she edged upward on the tips of her toes.

Sawyer's mouth hovered millimeters from her own. Her heart hammered. Her arms drifted and locked around his neck.

What was he waiting for? If he didn't go ahead and kiss her, she was going to fall over.

An electric bolt went through her the moment his lips touched hers.

The rough calluses of his palms cupped her face. His mouth broke free, his eyes holding her with his gaze, something powerful passing between them.

A catch in her breath, she kissed him back. Too soon—for Honey's preference—he released her. She leaned against the newel post, grateful for its support. She was glad to note he seemed to be having as much trouble recovering his breath as she.

She grasped for the threads of her composure. She mustn't let him see how he'd rattled her. "See? Just as I suspected."

He stilled, then with great deliberation passed his hand over his Coastie buzz cut. "I guess you showed me," he rasped.

Oh yeah, she'd shown him. Shown him how much she despised him.

Honey forced out a hollow laugh. "Just a walk down memory lane. Keeping it fun. Gotta keep the past in the past, though."

The bleakness in his eyes chilled her. "Right. What future could there have ever been between a messed-up cowboy Coastie and the Eastern Shore's Sweetheart?"

"Mission accomplished." Her mouth trembled. "And nobody calls me sweetheart."

Sawyer hooded his eyes, but not before she spotted the hurt there. Hurt she'd placed there. "Despite what you believe, Beatrice, I don't play games."

He staggered toward the door. "I'm going out to the truck to bring in some supplies." He hesitated at the entrance. "I hope we can still be friends."

Why did that leave her feeling empty?

Mission accomplished, all right. Instead of excising the Coastie from her life, the opposite had occurred. How was she going to keep her heart intact working alongside Sawyer to rebuild the inn? 'Cause kissing Sawyer Kole *had* proven to be as great as she'd remembered.

She sank onto the bottom step of the stairs. Truth be told, more so.

Chapter Thirteen

By the time she arrived at the lodge the next day, Honey had regained control of her mixed-up, messed-up emotions. Sort of.

Taking a deep breath, she plodded past the churned mud that used to be the lawn and stopped at the sight of a blue Chevy pickup backed to the porch, tailgate down. She jolted as ripping sounds overrode the raucous cry of the seagulls swooping over the sunlit, diamond-studded tidal creek. Piles of drywall littered the yard.

Inside the house, hammer raised, Sawyer paused when her shadow fell across the threshold. But he kept the hardened muscles of his back to her. "Grab a sledgehammer from the toolbox, Beatrice."

Expecting him to object to her continued participation, she'd prepared a speech. She itched to tell him off, but he'd stolen her thunder. "How'd you know it was me?"

His mouth did that curious, one-sided smile thing. "I always know when it's you."

She sashayed to the toolbox and brandished a hammer. "Okay. What do I do now?"

His eyes flitted from her black flats to her leggings to her pink blouse and tank top. "You're not really dressed for construction, Beatrice."

She lifted her chin. "Just because you remodel doesn't mean you can't do it with style. And I've been thinking." Honey ignored his groan. "We've been going about this the wrong way."

"Going about what?"

She fluttered her hand. "This thing between you and me."

His lips flattened. "I thought we put that to rest yesterday with the kiss that wasn't as great as you remembered."

She flushed. "I didn't say that."

He sighed. "What do you mean then?"

"I think instead of avoiding each other, we should go with the idea of more, not less, time spent together."

He cocked his head. "On the theory of yours that we'll get each other out of our systems?"

"Exactly."

"Let me see if I can get this through my thick, Coastie skull. You hate my guts, but now you want to spend more time with me?" He crossed his arms across his chest. "Seriously?"

Honey had a hard time keeping her gaze from following the ripple of his muscle. She swallowed. "Seriously." She worried her lower lip with her teeth. "And I don't hate you. You said you hoped we could be friends."

If anything, his mouth thinned further.

His silence unnerved her.

"I—I hope we can be friends, too." She took a step closer. "And friends spend time together, right? No harm, no foul."

He studied her. She twisted the pearl strand at her throat. He blew out a breath and unfolded his arms.

"Whatever you want, Beatrice. Have it your way." He flicked his eyes at her. "You always do anyway. Let's get to work."

She nodded, gulping past the inexplicable fear he'd refuse her olive branch. Friends… She could do friends.

Couldn't she?

He pointed his hammer at the watermark above the light switch. "Everything must be ripped out to that line." He rolled his tongue in his cheek. "Shouldn't be too difficult. Just imagine the wall is my head and give it a good whack." He smashed the wall with his hammer to demonstrate.

She winced, but feet spread hip-width in a girly-girl version of the regulation stance the guard had perfected, she braced. Raising the hammer above her head and using every ounce of her strength, she drove the hammer into the wall.

Honey staggered as the hammer bit through the soggy wall with far more force than necessary. Her arms vibrated. She glared at him over her shoulder. "Don't you dare laugh at me, Coastie."

Sawyer kept his face blank. But his shoulders quivered suspiciously. "I wouldn't dream of laughing. I'm more stunned than anything. Beatrice and a hammer? Who'd have thunk?" He shook his head. "But for safety's sake, I think I'll move out of range for my own protection."

Honey heaved the hammer with both hands above her head like she was employing the anvil at the Wachapreague Fireman's Carnival. "Might be the best decision you could make." She angled toward another section of the living room. "For your own safety."

"You're the boss."

She sniffed. "Most sensible thing I've ever heard come out of your mouth, cowboy." She grunted, striking at the drywall.

Within an hour, her arms ached with fatigue. He relieved her of the hammer and suggested she speed the process along by hauling drywall chunks to the growing pile outside. She suspected he'd invented the job to go easy on her. But after several backbreaking trips lugging drywall outdoors, she decided he hadn't done her any favors. By afternoon's end, they'd cleared everything from the living room and kitchen.

"Won't take long to remove the sections in the dining room." He leaned over, resting his hands on his knees. "After that, we'll have to dry everything out with industrial fans."

Sawyer straightened and stretched. At the glimpse of his muscles flexing, she had a hard time remembering to breathe.

After grabbing a bottle of water, he threw his head back and chugged.

This "working each other out of our system" wasn't working exactly as she'd envisioned. "Braeden said he found a generator."

He swallowed and swiped his mouth with the back of his hand. "From a fellow Coastie up Delaware way. The Coastie network is broad and vast."

She traced a circle in the dust-covered floor with the toe of her now-grimy flats. She'd know to come better dressed tomorrow. Stud finding yesterday had proven more fun and less dirty than attacking drywall today.

Her cheeks flushed at the memory of Sawyer kissing her. Friends, she reminded her pounding heart. "What about after we dry everything out?"

"Now that the Bay Bridge is open again, I've put a call in to a Coastie friend of mine who's a licensed electrician across the Bay. He'll replace the wiring and outlets in the walls."

"And what do we do about the HVAC system?" She batted her lashes. "Betcha didn't know I knew that word, did you?"

Sawyer rubbed the kinks out of his neck. "You never fail to surprise me, Beatrice."

Honey fisted her hands against the urge to touch him. "Truer words, I expect, were never spoken."

Sawyer laughed and relaxed his stance. But just as suddenly, his face shuttered, and he moved away. "I'd better go. You, too. It'll be dark soon."

Honey blinked. He was leaving already? Before she thought, she caught hold of his hand. "The church ladies have opened the fellowship hall to everyone for dinner. Grapevine says Miss Jean made her famous chicken casserole." She threw him a long look. "You should come."

Sawyer raised his brow at her fingers wound in his. "Do *you* want me to come?"

Honey let go. "Max would love to spend time with you."

"Would he be the only one who enjoys spending time with me?"

"What do you call what we've been doing all afternoon?"

"Making amends?" Breaking eye contact, he scrubbed his hand over his face. "Anyway, I got stuff to do. See you tomorrow?"

Stuff? What kind of stuff?

Frowning, she pursed her lips. "I'll be here."

His mouth curved. "Well, if demolishing drywall with you is the best I can do, I guess I'll take it." He gathered and notched the tool belt around his waist.

Out on the porch, he locked and secured the new door. Then Sawyer escorted her to her dad's truck and made sure the engine turned over before heading toward his new Chevy. He gave her a small wave as he slid behind the wheel.

Honey sighed as their trucks parted ways at the top of the Duer drive on Seaside Road. Glancing in the rearview mirror, she watched his taillights disappear in the direction of Onley. She deflated in the seat.

Tomorrow felt like a long, long time from now.

And it hadn't escaped her notice that he'd left another fresh bouquet of brown-eyed Susans on the mantel for her.

Over the next two weeks, Sawyer showed Honey how to insulate the exterior walls. He installed the subflooring himself. And he supervised Seth, the ROMEOs and other church volunteers in rehanging the drywall on the ground floor. But he waited till Honey took Amelia for an obstetrician appointment one afternoon before ripping away the damaged mantel and removing it from the premises.

The remodel was slowly but surely taking shape as September rolled into October. Nearing completion. Every day looking more and more like Honey's beloved home. Although this friend thing was slowly but surely killing him. When he longed for so much more.

Friends… He reminded himself at least six times an hour. Friends was a whole lot better than the nothing he'd had of Honey for the past three years. And for someone like him, it was better than he deserved or could reasonably expect.

He also made time for a trip to a lumber yard near Salisbury, Maryland. On the way he visited Mr. Keller in the rehab facility, too, who gave him permission to use some carving tools he'd found in the barn loft.

Mr. Keller, wheelchair bound with both legs casted, was lonely. Sawyer could tell the energetic senior citizen with the thick Eastern Shore brogue enjoyed their visit. Childless, the old man regaled Sawyer with tales of times on the farm nestled next to the sea when the Kellers raised horses the prize of many a Northern steel magnate. He found himself telling Mr. Keller about his childhood and the bronco circuit. Sawyer made it a habit to drop by and chat every other day.

Sawyer also surprised Honey with a toolkit of her own. With a quick upward sweep of her lashes, she opened the lid and examined the contents. He could tell she wanted to smile, but wouldn't allow herself.

"What's this for?"

"Figured you'd earned the right to your own tools, Beatrice."

He'd pleased her, but she'd never admit that out loud, least of all to him.

She hefted the screwdriver in her hand. "How come you know so much about construction, Sawyer?"

"Hidden talents. There's more to this Coastie than just a pretty face."

She rolled her eyes. As he'd meant her to. "Let me rephrase. Where did a bronco-busting, puddle pirate, speed demon adrenaline junkie learn construction?"

He smiled, arms folded, and rocked on his heels.

She wagged the tool in his face. "Would you get serious and answer my question? I'm trying to have an adult conversation with you, Kole."

He dropped his arms and returned to remeasuring the length of the window for the trim he needed to cut outside on the miter saw he'd set up in the yard. "My last foster dad was a contractor by trade. We were expected to help when school let out for the summer."

"Free labor?"

"Something like that. Pop Larsen wanted to make sure we learned a trade." He couldn't resist the chance to make her laugh. "Anyway, I've been told I'm good with my hands."

Her lips twitched as if she fought the urge to break into a smile. "Arrogant much, Kole?"

He could also tell he was wearing away her indifference—which was far worse than her resistance in his opinion.

Sawyer grinned at her. "Resistance is futile, baby."

"Don't call me that. I'm not your baby nor anyone

else's." She tightened the ponytail on the nape of her neck. "Once this remodel is done, we can finally get back to our real lives."

"Be careful what you wish for, Beatrice."

With a derisive lift of her eyebrow, she moved to the dining room where her dad had installed the new baseboards.

Sawyer got a kick out of seeing her jeans get holes in the knees from hard work and not from a New York designer. She was determined to prove she was more than just a pretty face. But he'd known that about her immediately when they crossed paths three years ago at the Sandpiper where she'd waitressed.

Now at the lodge, he stayed on the lookout every time she attempted a task on the remodel. Making sure it wasn't too heavy or hazardous. Stepping in to shift the load when she tackled more than she could handle.

He had to be smart about it, though. Not make it seem as if he was hovering or rushing to her rescue. She would hate that and resent him even more. But he kept a watchful eye on her at the construction site nonetheless.

Because remodel or not, he would've done that anyway. Every time she got in his range of vision, his antennae went on high alert, and his pulse kicked up a notch. The Honey effect, he called it.

She returned the next day with the side of her toolbox covered in spangled letters reading Handy Honey. And if anyone could put shine and sparkle into a dull, metallic toolkit, Honey was the one for the job.

With the mantel gone, Honey contemplated the fresh bouquet of wildflowers deposited by Sawyer on the seat of her dad's truck. Dad kept promising a trip to the mill to pick out a replacement, but so far finishing touches were the last things on everyone's minds.

Except perhaps for Sawyer. Who never failed to bring brown-eyed Susans to the worksite. Every day, another bouquet. She sighed. Only Sawyer would attempt to woo her—if that's what this was—with ditch flowers and a toolbox.

Was it working? Maybe…

They were supposed to be friends only. But the more time she worked alongside Sawyer Kole, the less friendly she felt. Instead, she felt… She gritted her teeth. *Not going there.*

She didn't know where Sawyer got his energy. She didn't know when he slept, either. As far as she could determine, his days were spent on shift at the station or organizing a team of volunteers from a North Carolina sister church who'd driven to the Delmarva Peninsula this weekend to lend a hand in the repositioning of the steeple.

She parked outside the Sandpiper, leaving the truck for her dad when he returned from an early morning fishing expedition. A few of his die-hard customers had returned for the excellent deep-sea fall fishing. Unfortunately, they were staying at a chain motel on the highway, not the Duer Lodge, which wasn't yet open for business.

Honey glanced around the bustling square on this mid-October day. The American and Coast Guard flags were aflutter atop the twin poles at the Coastie station. She shaded her hand over her eyes, gazing out across the harbor toward the barrier islands.

It was a gusty day. Dad, a seasoned waterman, would know to take it easy. But with the stiff wind, the repositioning of the steeple scheduled for today would have to wait.

Braeden promised to give her a ride back to Pauline's when he got off duty. She glanced at the time on her cell phone. Still a half hour. She'd finished the landscaping project around the lodge earlier than she'd imagined.

Come summer, the air would be heady with the smell of gardenias.

Might as well get a Long John and a coffee while she waited. The bells over the cafe door jingled as she strode inside. Waving to a few patrons she'd known since she was a child, she ordered from the counter. Dixie poured her a cup of coffee. Carrying the mug, Honey snagged a booth overlooking the village green.

Sipping the aromatic coffee, her gaze riveted to the activity centered around the church. The roof had been reshingled early in the aftermath of the storm by the same North Carolina men's ministry who'd returned this Saturday to correct the tilt of the steeple. Too bad they'd made the trip north for nothing, thanks to the weather.

No surprise it was Sawyer who snared her attention first and foremost among the throng of volunteer workers.

He clamped the strap of a hardhat underneath his chin. Another worker helped him step into and adjust a safety harness. She frowned. What was he—?

She set the porcelain mug with a thud onto the tabletop as she watched Sawyer's climb to the top of the church scaffolding. Her eyes darted to the flagpole across the square as a brisk wind snapped the fabric taut before her gaze cut to Sawyer. Losing his footing, his handhold on the iron bars slipped.

He fell and swung out over nothingness.

She sucked in oxygen, her heart in her throat. But the crane supporting the safety harness held. Dangling, Sawyer readjusted his grip, regained his footing and commenced with the repair work.

Her breath came in short, rapid gasps. "Of all the stupid… What are you trying to prove, Kole?" She clenched her teeth. "Anything for a thrill, eh?"

"Is that why you think Sawyer's working so hard?"

She jerked at Braeden's voice at the end of the booth.

She rested her hands palm down on the table. "I think he craves danger the way some people crave drugs."

Braeden burrowed his brow. "He's working two days on, and on his two days off, he's either at the Keller farm or your house. Weekends he works at the church."

He slid into the booth across from her. "Want me to tell you why I think Sawyer's pushing himself so hard?"

She pursed her lips. "Why do I feel you're going to tell me anyway?"

"I think Sawyer drives himself because he's trying to prove something to himself. And most of all, to you."

Her eyebrows rose. "To me?"

Braeden's eyes flitted toward the sound of the crane poised over the steeple. "Sawyer didn't abandon you that night on the beach in Ocean City. He waited in the shadows of the convenience store across the street until someone came for you. He reckoned you'd call Amelia. Only he didn't know I'd come, too, and confront him."

"He stayed?" She tried to wrap her mind around this new piece of information. "Why? What did he say to you, Braeden?"

Braeden's gaze dropped to the paper placemat. "Sawyer's been told his whole life he's a screw-up. He realized his life was on the wrong path. And he cared enough for you he didn't want to take you down with him."

Her mouth tightened. "He told me I wasn't the kind of girl he wanted."

"Sawyer didn't want to ruin your life." Braeden sighed. "I'll grant you his methods were brutal, but effective. He believed then it was only a matter of time before he ended up like his birth parents, and he loved you enough to cut you loose."

Honey shook her head. "Love me? He told you he loved me?" She made a face. "Funny how he's never said those words to me. I'm not sure that man knows the meaning of love."

Braeden's mouth hardened. "He was thinking about your happiness, not his. Took guts and courage to walk away from you. A sacrificial love that put his heart on the right path to eventually find God. He's become a fine young man who I'm proud to serve with." Braeden's eyes bored into her. "But more than that, I'm honored to call him my friend."

Friend… She was about sick of that word. "Why are you only telling me this now?"

Braeden leaned against the cracked vinyl upholstery. "I'm praying at last you've room in your heart to listen. To hear the truth. I think he's found peace for the first time in his life. A joy that can only come from God."

"How nice for him." She gripped the handle of the mug. "Glad to know one of us is happy."

A muscle ticked in Braeden's jaw. "The church is the heart of Kiptohanock, a place Sawyer holds dear. Possibly the first real place Sawyer's ever considered home. His happiness right now comes in using his skills to re-erect the steeple."

She knotted her fingers in her lap. "If he doesn't get himself killed first."

"As for the lodge?" Braeden glanced out the window again. "The lodge is your dearest dream, Honey. And for Sawyer, his greatest happiness lies in making you happy. Giving you back the home you love."

Braeden let out a gust of air. "Can't you see it, Honey? See his heart? Must you have the words in order to believe? He's not an eloquent man, not comfortable with words. He's showing you his love in a thousand different ways through his actions."

I'm good with my hands… That much he'd said to her a month ago. Was it true what Braeden supposed?

Chemistry she and Sawyer had in spades, but beyond that? They'd need far more than sparks to make it work between them if they wanted a chance for real, lasting love.

And the most fundamental of love's building blocks—trust. Chemistry was one thing. Trust was something entirely different.

Fool me once...

She fought the tears welling in her eyes.

"Here's a better question for you to ponder, Honey, instead of passing judgment." Braeden edged out of the booth. "Ever stop to wonder who takes care of Sawyer? Or if besides God, anyone ever did?"

Chapter Fourteen

Two days later, Honey eased the truck door open, trying not to startle Sawyer.

Head reclined against the seat, he didn't stir, a testimony to how tired he really was. She winced at the sight of the bandage wrapped around his forearm where he'd burned himself on a SAR mission earlier that afternoon. Sawyer wasn't careless. He was exhausted.

And just because she could, she allowed herself the luxury of studying his features.

Shadows smudged the skin beneath his closed lids. Grooves of weariness etched the corners of his mouth. There were deep hollows beneath his sharp cheekbones.

A brown leather Bible lay open on the seat beside him. She wondered what he'd been reading. And if it gave him the peace Braeden claimed Sawyer now possessed.

Peace… Honey was sinking—drowning—beneath a load of bitterness. An anger that had begun with the death of her mother, stoked by Caroline's inexplicable desertion and punctuated by Lindi's death.

As for Sawyer's complete and utter rejection? The icing on the cake. But his motivation? Perhaps not what she'd believed three years ago. There were a lot of things she was starting to reconsider.

She let out a small, hopeless sigh. If she had her druthers, she'd stand here all day and look at him. But this time, the rescuer needed a little rescuing of his own. And she was just the woman for the job.

"Wake up, Sawyer," she whispered. "Wake up."

He blinked and jerked upright. His hands grabbed for the wheel.

She touched his sleeve. "It's okay. You fell asleep in the truck. It's just me."

His eyes flickered from her to the dusky glow of approaching nightfall above the tree line. "There's no 'just you' about it, Beatrice."

Sawyer swallowed and reached for the key hanging in the ignition. "I didn't mean to hold you up. I better get going and check on Keller's horses."

"Wait..." She caught his arm. "You need to eat something first. Between the station, the steeple and the house, you're working too hard."

"The whole town's working hard to restore what was lost in time for Harbor Fest. Don't worry about me. I'm fine."

"You don't look fine. You look tired. Like you haven't had a decent meal in days. You're so busy taking care of everyone else, but who takes care of you?"

His hands flexed around the wheel. "I take care of myself."

She nudged her chin at the bandage. "And not doing a great job. Come inside the house. I brought you a plate of food."

He pushed back his shoulders. "Just give me the plate."

She wagged her finger at him. "Not happening, Kole. You'll scarf it down in between shoveling horse manure or cleaning tack. Not healthy. You need to take a break."

"I told you I'm fine. Got to keep moving. If I stop moving—"

"You fall asleep in your truck."

Sawyer flushed.

Honey planted her hands on her hips. "You're dead on your feet and no good to anyone if you don't get some rest. So get out of the vehicle, Coastie. Don't make me go all steel magnolia on you. I promise, you wouldn't like it."

"Steel gardenia in your case." His eyes teased. "Don't sell yourself short, Beatrice. I think maybe I would."

Honey's knees buckled at the unrepentant buccaneer grin he shot her way. And she made a quick grab for the support of the truck door. Gardenias… So he'd noticed. Her "little" landscaping project had evolved into lots of old-fashioned shrubs—gardenias, lilacs and hydrangeas.

And she'd developed more than a little fondness for ditch daisies.

With her heart jackhammering, she reminded herself of her mission objective. "We can do this the easy way or the hard way. Your choice." An echo of his words to her on the day of the storm.

She cocked her head. "But one way or the other, cowboy, you're coming inside the house and eating the food."

His lips curved. "You gonna force feed me, Beatrice?"

She placed her foot on the truck's running board. "Whatever it takes. Besides, there's a few painting ideas I want to run by you."

"More on the Honey Do-er list?" Mock-groaning, he let go of the wheel. "So you want a design consult?"

Actually, not so much. The trick, she'd decided long ago in dealing with the male species, was knowing when and how much steel versus gardenia to apply. She switched to a more cajoling tone.

"I'd also prefer not to eat alone." She looked down and then up at him out of the corner of her eyes. "Keep me company while I eat, Sawyer?"

He raked his hand over his Coastie cut. "I—I didn't realize you hadn't eaten..."

She caught his hand, his palm warm against hers. Indulging in the tiny frisson of pleasure his touch wrought. Even with his off duty construction attire of jeans and T-shirt, Honey was still so Coastie-susceptible.

Okay...maybe not so much Coastie-susceptible as Sawyer-susceptible.

As Sawyer gave her hand a squeeze and swung his legs out of the truck, she stepped aside to give him room. To her chagrin, he let go of her hand.

He swept his arm toward the rebuilt screened porch. "Lead on, O fearless Duer."

She sniffed. "Like you once told me, better be careful what you wish for, Kole."

"Bossy much, Beatrice?"

She arched a look at him over her shoulder. "I'm not bossy, Coastie. I've got leadership skills."

Wrenching open the screen door, Sawyer's laughter made her grin. Wouldn't do to let him know that, though.

Inside the kitchen, Sawyer watched her unwrap the foil off a paper plate. She'd placed the ditch daisies he'd left—like the pitiful, lovesick XPO he was—in an antique blue bottle vase, he noted. She moved the flowery rays of sunshine to the kitchen windowsill overlooking the marsh.

"There." Honey angled. "It'll catch the last rays of light."

She handed him a plastic fork. "You'll have to eat standing up."

He leaned against the newly installed countertop. "Where's yours?"

She shrugged. "We can share."

It was hard being this close to her every day. Working

alongside Honey, yet never being able to—Sawyer jabbed the fork into the pile of mashed potatoes.

He closed his eyes and moved his lips in a quick prayer. He opened them to find her watching him this time, her arms crossed. Dropping his gaze, he shoveled the potatoes into his mouth.

Sawyer's mouth watered, and he realized he couldn't remember the last time he ate. Probably those Long Johns Reaves brought to the station that morning. And before that?

Half a plate later, Sawyer froze, the fork suspended midway to his mouth. "I forgot to share." He put down the fork. "Sorry." He pushed the plate across the plastic-swathed granite toward Honey.

A smile quirked her lips. "I'm not. You were hungry. I like watching a man enjoy his food."

"I always enjoy your food, Hon—" He caught himself. "Beatrice."

Her smile dimmed. She shoved the plate back at him. "Go ahead and finish it."

"But you—"

"I'm not as hungry as I thought. I'll grab something at Miss Pauline's."

His brows knit, but he grabbed the biscuit and took a bite. She whirled in a slow three-sixty, taking in the reconstructed commercial kitchen. At her happiness, a satisfaction filled long empty places inside him.

She'd decided on a French country design—off-white cabinets, a yellow-and-blue-tiled backsplash, and touches of warm reds. She dreamed. He implemented.

Which, in *his* dreams, was how it ought always to be between him and Honey.

"It's going to be better than it was before thanks to you, Sawyer."

He concentrated on taking the next bite. And chewing

some more. He made a deliberate effort to swallow. "I promised you I'd give you your home back and I meant it."

"What was your home like, Sawyer?"

He choked. Coughed. And stalled. "Oklahoma. You know that. Rodeo and barns. Now the Guard."

"I meant your home as a boy."

He dropped the biscuit. He so did not want to go there. Not with her.

She fingered the strand of pearls at her throat. "You've never told me about your parents. What were they like?"

He concentrated on placing the fork across the width of the plate just so.

"Sawyer… Talk to me."

At her hushed tone, he glanced up.

Her face gentled. "Please…"

Shuffling his feet on the yet to be varnished hardwood pine, he wiped his hands along the side of his jeans. Might as well get this over with. In a few weeks, with the remodel of the church and inn complete, it wouldn't matter if she knew.

"My mother died on the streets from a drug overdose. My father died in prison for an armed bank robbery gone wrong."

Her eyes widened.

"Great gene pool, huh?" Curling his lip, he stuffed his hands in his pockets. "Never had a real family. The Larsens were the closest, court-ordered guardians I ever got."

Honey inserted her arm through the crook of his elbow. "So you modeled yourself after them. Became a guardian of the sea."

Something pinged in his chest. Funny how Honey Duer got him. Sometimes better than he understood himself. And her sweetness, so like the old Honey, threatened to undo the careful barricades he'd erected around his heart.

He played off her words, allowing his shoulder to rise

and fall. "Sounds much more noble than what I actually thought as an eighteen-year-old recruit after graduating from the system with nowhere else to go."

It hurt his heart to contemplate what she must think of him. But being Honey, she once again surprised him.

"So they abandoned you? Kicked you out? How long were you with them?" Her brown eyes flashed. "How old were you when you were placed the first time?"

"Ten." He frowned at the intensity in her gaze, confused by the anger in her voice. "I was with the Larsens only during high school."

Was she angry with him? Angry with the Larsens? Why was she angry at all?

"The Larsens are good people. But there were other kids, a long line, waiting for the same chance they'd given me. It's the way the system works. They've tried to stay in touch. Phone calls, cards, but—"

"But you let them in too far, regretted it and rebuilt your walls. Kind of a pattern with you, isn't it? Leave before they leave you."

A beat of silence.

Sawyer stared at her. "I guess it is."

Her eyes softened. "Lessening the chances of being hurt. Not allowing yourself to be vulnerable. Has this strategy worked?"

"Until I met you..." He gulped past the boulder clogging his throat. "Yeah, it did."

Chapter Fifteen

Honey's heart accelerated at his words. Her eyes drifted to the blue vase of ditch daises on the windowsill. If what he'd said was true, she and Sawyer weren't that different in the way they coped with life's wounds.

Except she coped alone. And Sawyer had found a God who'd promised to never forsake him.

Her strategy involved keeping everyone at arm's length behind the veneer of her invincible hospitality. The always in control Hostess with the Mostest. And her strategy had worked so well. Until a certain cowboy Coastie sailed back into her life.

She bit her lip. "What was the verse you were reading in the truck?"

He avoided her gaze. "You mean before I fell asleep?"

"It appeared well-worn to that spot in your Bible."

Sawyer propped his elbows on the countertop and hunched over the plate. "Sometimes I forget that verse is meant for me, too. So I have to read it over and over. I get enormous peace from that verse."

Hoping he'd trust her with another piece of his heart, she held her breath. Baby steps. Patience. Neither of them—*God help them both*—were the trusting sort.

He scrunched the aluminum foil into a ball. "It's from Romans."

She exhaled.

He took a jump shot into the oversized construction trashcan. "'Therefore there is no condemnation for those in Christ Jesus.'"

Condemnation. Her chest tightened. Is that what he felt from her? She'd no right to judge Sawyer. She was only just beginning to understand the challenges he'd faced in his life.

Her cell phone rang. She fished it out of her jean pocket and read the text. "Oh, no."

"What's wrong?"

"It's from Braeden. Amelia's in labor again. They're at Riverside."

Sawyer frowned. "Is it still too early? Are she and the baby okay?"

"It's Max Braeden's worried about. I need to go to Riverside and take care of Max while Braeden's with Amelia. Dad's stuck in Salisbury on a supply run with one of the ROMEOs."

Sawyer tossed the paper plate and plastic utensils in the trashcan. "I'll drive you."

"You don't have—"

"Max and I are buddies." The hinges of the screen door squeaked as he held it for Honey. "Besides, I want to be there for him—and for you."

"Thank you." Her mouth trembled. "I don't feel quite up to making the trek alone anyway."

She waited in his truck while he did a quick check to make sure the doors were secure. He slid behind the wheel. "Don't worry. Max will be okay." He steered the Chevy toward the hospital at Nassawadox.

Honey gripped the armrest. "The hospital holds bad

memories for Max. It's where he endured so much pain during the fight to save his life from the leukemia."

"We'll both be there for him."

She massaged her throbbing temples. "This baby has brought out insecurities in Max none of us suspected. He thinks once the baby arrives, Braeden and Amelia won't love him anymore. Silly, I know, but—"

"Not so silly." Sawyer's mouth flattened. "He feels alone and he's scared. He needs to know he's deeply loved."

Sawyer's eyes cut across the cab to her and then onto the road. "I know about feeling scared and alone."

Honey looked at him for a long moment. Seeing him. Feeling the deep, understated hurts in his soul.

"I'm guessing you would," she whispered.

The bright florescent lights and pungent antiseptic smells hit Honey as soon as the hospital doors slid open. They found Max in the care of a nurse in the waiting room. Hunkered in an armchair, his feet dangled, not quite long enough to touch the floor.

Sawyer strode forward. "Max."

The little boy shot out of the chair. Bypassing Honey, he flew in a straight trajectory to Sawyer.

Sawyer went down on one knee and opened his arms. With a small cry, Max's arms went around Sawyer's neck. Sawyer enfolded the child in his embrace.

Honey brushed her hand across Max's cheek. Max loosened his hold on Sawyer and dragged her into the circle of their embrace. "It's going to be okay." She rubbed Max's back. "We're here now."

"I want my Mimi," Max whispered. "'Spose the baby kills her like I…?" He buried his face in Sawyer's shirt.

"That's not true, Max." She cradled the crown of Max's head. "Is that what this has been about?"

Sawyer lugged the three of them over to the sofa. "You didn't kill your mother. That's not what happened."

"You don't know, Sawyer," Max sobbed. "You weren't there."

She touched his cheek. "But I was, Max. I was here in this very room the day you were born."

Max lifted his head. His eyes, like twin blueberries, swam with tears. "You were here?"

Honey nodded. "It was a drunk driver who killed your mom. Never you. Because Lindi loved you so much, she hung on so she could give you life. You are Lindi's last, most precious gift to us. She loved you. Mimi loves you. We all love you. And nothing and no one will ever change who you are to us."

Sawyer caught Max's chin between his thumb and forefinger. "Remember what you said the day after the storm? God made a way for Mimi to be your forever mom and for Braeden to become your dad. God's love is like that, too. His love doesn't decrease with every person born. It becomes more. And so it will be with Braeden and Mimi. I've learned if you open your heart, the love you give will flow right back to you. Even stronger."

Opening your heart. That was the trick, wasn't it? Trusting. Believing in a love like that. Whether in the love of God or in the love of an erstwhile Coastie.

The anger was far safer. She couldn't risk anything more. Not and retain control of her emotions. As long as she had her family, her house and her business, she'd be fine. She so didn't need the complication of a Coastie in her life.

A nurse entered the waiting area distracting Honey. "It's a boy."

They rose as one.

"And my sister? Is she okay?"

Max slid from Sawyer's arms. "Mimi?"

The nurse gestured to the hallway. “Mother and child are doing great. If you’d like a sneak peek at the baby, they’re bringing him into the nursery for a few minutes while your sister is settled into a permanent room.”

She squatted to Max’s level. “You can visit your Mimi soon.” The nurse patted Max’s cheek. “What a great big brother you’re going to be.”

Honey took Max’s hand. The three of them followed the nurse down the long corridor to a glass-banked window. Bassinets lined the nursery. Filled with tiny, squirming, squalling, puckered, red-faced infants.

Pink or blue caps. Family names identified the bundles of joy. Colonna. Turner. Scott.

Max crinkled his nose. Although the noise was muted through the glass, the cacophony on the other side was almost visceral. “He looks loud.”

Her lips twitched. “Then you’ll be a matched pair. ’Cause you’re loud, too, Max.”

Max studied the baby. “Why’s he wrapped up like a burrito?”

Sawyer laughed.

“Hey, Max.”

They turned at the sound of the little redheaded girl’s voice. Honey tensed. Whenever these two crossed paths, there were fireworks. She and Sawyer exchanged dubious glances.

The little girl sidled next to Max and pressed her nose against the glass. “Which one is yours?”

Max pointed.

Shoulder-to-shoulder with him, the little girl sighed. “You’re so lucky.” A wistful note entered in her voice. “I wish I had a baby.”

Max turned his head from his contemplation of the baby and stared at her.

She kept her eyes riveted on the brawling mass of tiny

humanity on the other side of the glass. "You're going to be the best big brother ever."

Max's shoulders broadened. "Yes." His chest puffed out. "I am."

"Izzie..." Weston Clark hurried along the corridor. "I've been looking everywhere for you."

The little girl—Isabelle Clark—huddled closer to the window.

He glanced apologetically at Honey. "I'm so sorry, Miss Duer. I hope Izzie hasn't been intrusive. I was visiting a neighbor on the next ward over and she got away from me."

She patted Izzie's shoulder. "No problem. She and Max were just visiting his new baby brother."

Weston Clark's eyes darted around the white-walled hallway as if expecting structural breaches. Sawyer went into regulation stance. "Commander Clark, sir."

Clark shook his head. "Not in the service any more, Petty Officer. No need for protocol. I'm a Kiptohanock citizen now." He glanced at his daughter. "And Izzie's father full-time." He held out his hand. "Time to go home, Izzie."

Izzie molded her lips to the glass and blew a kiss at the babies, leaving a wet imprint of her mouth. "Bye, Max," she whispered and slipped her hand into her father's.

Max waved. "Bye, Izzie."

Braeden passed the Clarks and caught Max in his arms. "Hey, son. I've missed you."

Max peered over Braeden's shoulder into the nursery. "What's the new kid's name?"

Sawyer laughed.

Honey play-slapped his arm. "Don't encourage him."

"We're going to call him Patrick." Braeden's gaze flicked to Honey. "Patrick Jordan Scott."

Her eyes watered. "Oh, Braeden. That's so kind of you."

Jordan—for Amelia's deceased fiancé, also Coast Guard, and Pauline Crockett's son.

Braeden swallowed. “Miss Pauline has been good to us. And her son loved Amelia.” A sheen gathered in his eyes. “I got the girl and an entire future with her. A small thing to do in his memory.”

Honey tilted her head. “Not small. And I’m thinking if the baby were a girl, my dear big sis wouldn’t be suggesting you call her Carly after *your* former fiancée.”

Braeden grinned and dashed the moisture from his eyes. “And rightly so. A noose I escaped just in time.” He planted a hand on Max’s shoulder. “Mimi can’t wait to see you.”

Max jabbed his finger at the glass and Baby Scott. “Is he going to be there, too?”

Braeden exchanged looks with Honey. “We thought maybe you’d like to spend time with us alone…before…”

Max frowned. “I don’t think my baby likes it in there with those screaming fish faces.”

Braeden’s eyebrows lifted. *My baby?* he mouthed.

She and Sawyer shrugged.

“I got a lot to teach the baby before I grow up.”

“Like?” Braeden prompted.

“Like how to find the best sea glass. Like how to cut bait for Granddad.” Max’s shoulders rose and fell. “Like how to go clamming and a hundred million trillion other fun stuff.”

“There’ll be plenty of time for it all.” Braeden urged Max away from the window. He stopped in front of Honey and Sawyer. “Thanks, you two, for being here for all of us.”

Sawyer smiled. “No problem.”

Max tugged on Braeden’s shirt. “P.J. looks like you, Dad.”

“P.J.?”

Max nodded. “Peanut butter and jelly.”

Braeden made a valiant attempt not to laugh. Sawyer didn’t even try to hold back. She punched him again.

Honey took another look into the nursery. Max was

right. Dark fuzz peeked from underneath the blue stocking cap. And when Patrick Jordan Scott wasn't bawling with his eyes screwed shut, they appeared a dark navy blue, which she guessed would turn into brown like Braeden's.

Braeden ruffled Max's hair. "He does. But you know how I've always loved redheads, son."

Max smiled for the first time and blew a breath between his lips. "Yeah, that's right."

He took Braeden's hand and pulled him forward. "And I'm going to be the best big brother in the world."

Watching them disappear into an elevator, she swiped at her eyes. But a desolation on Sawyer's face stabbed at her heart. She touched his arm. "What's wrong?"

"Nothing." He shook her off. "I think the really blessed one is Patrick Jordan Scott. Not everyone gets a great big brother like Max." He cleared the hoarseness from his throat.

The way he said it…

"Do you have a big brother, Sawyer?"

Sawyer's mouth tightened. "Closest I've ever come to a big brother is Braeden. I made a lousy big brother myself."

Her eyes widened. "You have a—?"

"Did have a sister." He grimaced. "And like everything else in my life, including you, I ruined that, too."

The pain in his eyes stole her breath.

"Everything I touch, I ruin."

"Sawyer, that's not—"

"Come on." He strode down the hallway. "I'll make sure you get home."

But her father met them in the hospital lobby, and Sawyer went to wherever it was he kept himself in his off duty hours alone. Staring at his hunched shoulders as he disappeared into the darkened parking lot, she suspected he'd spent far too much of his life exactly the same—alone.

And that thought made her heart ache to rush after him.

It had gutted her to hear him describe in such a studied nonchalance the life he'd endured as a boy. And what he hadn't bothered to voice—what his home life must have been like prior to coming under the care of Child Protective Services. She quaked to think of the fear and vulnerability ten-year-old Sawyer had experienced every time he was yanked from one foster home into another.

No wonder he'd learned to live in the moment, to yearn for the eight-second thrill or the adrenaline-packed life of a Coastie. Now was all he knew, all he ever dared hope for. She hadn't realized he'd been about the same age as she when her mother died.

But oh, the stark differences beyond that one similarity. She'd had her dad and Amelia to carry her through. He'd had no one, only himself to rely upon. She began to understand Sawyer believed he dared not reach for more. Worse still, that he didn't deserve more.

"Sawyer told me about his parents." She nudged her father toward the elevator. "Why didn't you tell me before, Dad?" The doors whooshed open.

Her father punched in the floor number on the keypad to the maternity wing. "It was his story to tell. The reason he walked away from you on that beach. He believed he was saving you. From himself." The doors closed.

"Everything he touches, he ruins… That's what he told me, Dad." Her voice broke. "It isn't true." The elevator ascended.

"But he believes it to be true and for him, that's his reality."

"Daddy…" She leaned her head against the stalwart form of her father. "He's going to leave again. As soon as the steeple and the inn are finished. Leave me again. What should I do?"

"What do you want to do, Honey? Do you want a future with him?" The elevator doors slid open.

If only she were brave enough to trust. Lindi had been brave. Max had faced his leukemia with bravery.

She followed her father out of the elevator. It had taken enormous courage for Amelia to finally let go of her fears and trust Braeden with her heart. Locating the correct room, her dad surged through the open door. He planted a quick kiss on Amelia, propped upright on pillows in the hospital bed.

Max stretched beside his Mimi on the bed cradling Baby Patrick in his arms. And bedside, Braeden guarded them both.

The little boy's eyes shone. "Look at me, Aunt Honey. I'm holding my baby. And P.J. smiled at me." He nuzzled his lips on Patrick's forehead.

She hung back in the doorway, gazing at Amelia's reward for faithfulness and trust.

There was nothing safe about loving Sawyer Kole. He was a landmine of emotional potholes. Unlike her safe, decoratively ordered world, he was messy. Potentially dangerous.

With him, she felt as if she stood on the brink of a high cliff. And she was barely holding on. With no safety net like he'd worn on the church scaffolding.

If she let go, if she relaxed for one minute, she'd fall off the edge. And then what? A free fall into nothingness?

Or unimaginable joy?

Chapter Sixteen

By late October everything was completed at the lodge. The appliances installed. The pine floors sanded and varnished. Everything done except for the finishing touches and painting the living room. The volunteers, the Coasties and the ROMEOs moved on to helping other neighbors.

And Sawyer stopped coming by. Though Honey never managed to catch him in the act, somehow he still managed to leave fresh ditch daises in the blue vase every day. One morning, she decided to go looking for him. But first, she took her hammer and went out to the porch for a little vandalism.

Not finding him at the station or the church—where the last coat of paint was being applied to the upright steeple—she ventured farther afield. Toward the Keller farm.

Driving through the iron gates at the entrance to the property, she breathed deeply of the crisp autumn air through the open window of her dad's truck. She gazed across the fallow fields and, to her relief, spotted Sawyer's truck parked between the hip-roofed Dutch barn and the two-story Victorian Sears, Roebuck & Company farmhouse. Pecan trees studded the yard.

It was pretty out here with the silver band of the channel shimmering through the tree cover. Keller and her dad had been friends for years, but she'd had no occasion to venture here since she was a girl when Mr. Keller used to open the farm for hayrides every spring. She parked in the barn's shadow and got out.

As she wandered into the open barn, filtered darkness engulfed her. Beams of light dappled the horse stalls. Horses snuffled. She was struck at how tidy everything was kept. The sharp tang of leather and the sweet scent of hay overlay more pungent odors. This was Sawyer's world, and she felt a rare privilege to catch a glimpse into an aspect of himself he often kept concealed.

Blankets hung over the side of the stalls. She peered into each at the bays and palominos. In the last stall, empty of horseflesh, she discovered where Sawyer had been sleeping in the aftermath of the storm.

She frowned at the cot and the black duffle she recognized as Sawyer's. Out here alone, except for the horses. Of all the stubborn, hardheaded…

Honey wrapped her arms around her navy blue jacket. The nights of late had grown chilly. Too cold to be out here. Why couldn't he have bunked in one of the spare rooms in the house?

But she already knew the answer to that. He didn't think he belonged. He didn't think himself deserving.

Honey turned on her heel and headed for the house. If he wasn't in the barn, he had to be somewhere. And her diligence was rewarded when she heard a squeaking valve shutting off a flow of water inside.

She yanked open the screen door. "Sawyer?" She stepped into the front hall.

Footfalls echoed across the wooden floor. Sawyer's eyes widened as he emerged from the rear of the house. "Beatrice? What are you doing here?"

Out of uniform now, he'd changed into jeans and a long-sleeved Western-cut shirt. But water glistened in his close-cropped hair. And she figured he'd come into the house to shower.

Sawyer stepped closer. "Is everything okay? Max? The baby? Your dad?"

Honey fluttered her hand. "Everybody's fine. Amelia and family are getting acquainted at Miss Pauline's and awaiting our re-occupancy of the Duer home."

Sawyer's eyes flickered to his boots. "Good."

Honey took a breath. "I haven't seen you around."

Sawyer shuffled his feet. "Been busy. The church steeple."

"Which, by the way, looks fantastic." She moistened her lips. "I need to finalize my color choices for the living room before the paint crew arrives on Tuesday. We move in on Thursday, just in time for Harbor Fest weekend."

An uncomfortable silence followed. This was not going the way she'd envisioned it in her head.

She tried again. "Wanted to get your opinion since the remodel has been so much your vision."

That got his attention. His eyes shot to hers, and he rocked on his heels. "More your vision than mine, Beatrice."

"Both of our visions. I looked for you in the barn—"

"You went in the barn?" He tensed.

She blinked. "Well, yes. When I couldn't find you at first—"

"You went into the loft?" He crossed his arms over his chest.

Honey shook her head. "I didn't think about searching there. I headed for the house."

Sawyer tightened his jaw. "Good."

His eyes drifted away before returning to meet her gaze. "So you drove all the way out here to ask me about paint chips?"

When he put it that way, it did seem ridiculous.

She jutted her hip. "I guess like Grandma Duer always said, a poor excuse is better than none."

A smile touched his lips. "You don't need an excuse to come see me, Beatrice."

"I didn't…" She blew out an exasperated breath. "It's not just the paint colors. Several of the railing spindles have come loose, and I wondered if you'd come by the house and fix them for me."

Sawyer cocked his head. "Come loose? How—?"

"Vandals." She bit her lip.

He gaped at her. "Someone vandalized the lodge? Was anything else damaged?"

She studied her shoes. "No… Not exactly."

He frowned. "This sounds like a job for your deputy sheriff boyfriend, Pruitt."

"Charlie's not my…" She glared at him. "This is a job for you, Sawyer. No need to involve the police." Her mouth flattened. "Will you come or not?"

His eyebrows rose. If he didn't know for a fact the painting was yet to be completed, he'd have sworn the fumes had addled her brain. "Sure, but I still say—"

"Can you come now?" She took hold of his sleeve and he allowed himself to be tugged toward the porch. The screen door banged shut behind them.

"Pushy much, Beatrice?" His eyes darted around the pasture. "I need to take care of the horses first. I'd planned on exercising at least one of them."

He set off across the yard. On second thought—

"Uh, Beatrice…" He pivoted so abruptly she plowed into his chest. Ricocheting, she stutter-stepped backward.

If he wasn't so intent on keeping her out of the barn, Sawyer would've laughed at the expression on her face.

"Why do you always—?" She choked off the rest of what she'd been about to say.

Because they both knew what she'd wanted to say. They both knew, because it was she who'd told him to call her Beatrice in the first place. And until she asked him—politely—to call her something else?

Sawyer's lips twitched. He persisted in calling her Beatrice mainly to get a rise out of her. Just cause he could. Plus, it was so much fun watching the cool, collected Beatrice "Honey" Duer go all steel gardenia on him.

Her mouth pursed—too kissable by far—in the effort, he figured, to bite her tongue.

"How about you wait on the porch?"

"Why can't I go with you?"

Sawyer gave her attire a quick perusal. The summer-white capris exchanged for dressy jeans 'cause girly-girls like Honey didn't wear white after Labor Day. Pearl studs adorned her earlobes. And she sported her usual high heels.

He rolled his tongue in his cheek. "Don't want to mess up your fancy shoes with horse poop."

She narrowed her eyes. "You trying to get rid of me or something? I haven't seen you in a week."

"I'm touched you noticed." He laid his hand over his heart. "Miss me, Beatrice?"

She growled. "Don't flatter yourself, Kole."

Actually, *he'd* missed *her*. No surprise there. But Harbor Fest was next weekend. And after that?

He'd reverted to his usual modus operandi—backing off in hopes of making it hurt less in the long run when he left the Shore for good.

But she was here now. His heart had leaped at the sound of her voice calling his name in the house. Perhaps going cold turkey with Honey wasn't such a good idea.

Why deny himself the pleasure of her company until he had to? Why not milk every ounce of joy while he had the chance? Soon enough, he'd leave for his next station in coastal North Carolina and never see her again.

He winced.

"What's wrong?"

"Nothing." He moved toward the barn. "If you're going to tag along, expect to be put to work, Beatrice."

She gave him a small salute. "Aye, aye, Petty Officer. Your wish is my command."

He snorted, sounding not unlike one of the horses. "That'll be the day."

"I could ride one of the horses, too. Help you out for a change."

He stopped in his booted tracks. "You want to go on a trail ride? With me?"

She tossed her hair over her shoulder. "Haven't seen Keller's farm in a long time. Why don't you give me the tour?"

He arched a brow. "At the risk of being slapped down again, you're hardly dressed for horseback riding."

"I'll manage somehow." And to show him she could, Honey kicked off her high-heeled pumps. She wiggled her merlot-painted toes in the grass.

"Please?" Those sunflower-brown eyes of hers bored into his. "One ride?"

His breath jammed in his throat. One ride, when all he wished for on God's earth was that it could be the first of many. But he'd lived long enough—and hard enough—to recognize a gift when offered. Sawyer might not be the sharpest tool in the chest, but he possessed enough sense to seize with both hands the joy of time spent in Honey's company.

Sawyer swallowed. "There's only one horse needs riding right now. Vet's got Alfalfa on restriction for a few days. Spanky and Buckwheat got a workout yesterday."

Her eyes enlarged. "Mr. Keller named his horses after the Little Rascals?"

Sawyer bit back a smile. "He did."

"Wait." She put her hand on her hip. "One horse? You want me to ride in the saddle with you?"

He rubbed the stubble on his jaw and waited for her to refuse.

She tucked a wisp of hair behind her ear. His eyes followed her hand. Awareness rippled between them.

Honey dropped her hand to her side. "Okay..." she whispered.

Sawyer saddled the horse in record time. Before she had a chance to change her mind. After leading Froggy into the yard, he stuck one foot into the stirrup and swung his leg over. The leather groaned as he settled into the saddle. He leaned forward over the saddle horn, inhaling the rich scents of hay and horse.

Honey must have caught him because she smiled up at him. "This smells good to you, doesn't it?"

Kicking one boot free of the stirrup, he extended his hand. "Yup. Put your foot there and I'll haul you the rest of the way."

"Haul?" She grunted as he heaved her upward. "You make me sound so...less than elegant."

Sawyer edged back on the mare, making room. "Ready?"

Her eyes glinted. "*Semper paratus*, Coastie. Always."

Sawyer held her steady, and positioned her in front of him. She teetered, almost unseating them both. "Easy there, Girly-Girl."

Honey grabbed for the saddle horn. "I'd forgotten what a long way it is to fall."

Sawyer wrapped his arms around her, taking the reins. He clicked his tongue against his teeth. Froggy rocked into motion. She gasped.

He tightened his hold around her waist. "I'd never let you fall." His mouth brushed against her hair. "And if you did fall, I'd catch you, I promise."

Sawyer breathed in the signature fragrance of her hair. Gardenias, the only scent in his opinion that topped horses and hay. Bypassing the rundown corral, he steered the horse toward the rim of trees.

At the easy rhythm of the horse, she gradually relaxed her stiff posture and leaned into him for support. His heart went into overdrive.

"It's beautiful here."

Sawyer pulled the reins taut and rested Froggy at the top of an incline with grand views of the farm on one side and the tidal creek beyond the sloping bank. "I wish there'd been a place like this for me and Cotton when we were kids." He clamped his lips together at his inadvertent admission.

Honey twisted in the saddle. "Cotton? Is that your sister?"

Sawyer heaved a sigh. "My little sister. Towheaded—so I called her Cotton."

Honey's mouth quirked. "You do love the nicknames, don't you, Coastie?"

At her choice of words, he laughed. "Appears I'm not the only one."

She smiled. "Would you tell me about your sister? Please?"

Holding the reins loosely, he struggled for an even tone before he found the courage to speak. "She had sky blue eyes."

"Like yours." Honey touched his cheek with her hand.

Sawyer nestled for a moment in the warmth of her palm. "Hers were a tad darker, I think. She was sweet and quiet." He frowned. "Too quiet. So as not to draw Dad's anger when he was on one of his drunks."

"What happened to her, Sawyer?"

Angling out of reach of her hand, he faced the water. "I don't know. I was ten when my dad was arrested for armed robbery and went to prison. Cotton was five. Mom left us when she was three. I'm not sure Cotton remembered her." He shrugged. "Probably better that way. There's a lot of things I wish I could forget."

"Why were you separated?"

He really didn't want to have this conversation with her. He'd spent the greater portion of his life trying to put it behind him. Not dwelling on situations that couldn't be fixed.

Sideways in the saddle, she rested her cheek against the fabric of his shirt and twined her arms around his torso. "You don't have to tell me if you don't want to. But after what you said at the hospital, I wondered. It hurts me how much you hurt as a boy."

And he found himself telling Honey what he'd never told another soul. How Child Protective Services took them from the hovel they'd called home when their father went to jail. How after a temporary emergency foster placement, he and his sister were separated.

The shy, little kindergartner with the flyaway hair was easily adopted. He, the angry, hardheaded preteen, went to a series of foster homes.

"She found her forever home." He gulped. "I never did."

His gaze roamed over the top of Honey's head and across the tidal marsh. Not till he met Honey Duer. Loved and lost his chance with her. Letting Honey, like Cotton and so many other good things, slip through his fingers.

"I can't understand how they could separate you." Honey's breath billowed against his neck. "If I hadn't had my sisters…"

He brushed his mouth across the silkiness of her hair. "I tried to find her once I turned eighteen and joined the Guard. But the adoption records were sealed. Her adoptive parents changed her name, of course. I had no idea who they were or where they were from."

Sawyer closed his eyes, reliving that heart-wrenching

period after he left the security of the Larsen foster ranch. “I put out information on one of the websites that reunites adoptees with their birth family. But no luck. After a while, I moved around so much with the Guard I stopped looking. She’s probably better off without a brother like me anyway.”

Honey stiffened. “I don’t believe that and neither should you. And don’t you dare say those you touch you ruin.

Sawyer’s eyes flew open.

Honey captured his face between her hands. “If I ever hear you say that again, Sawyer Kole, I’m going to be forced to take drastic action.”

Sawyer’s mouth curved. “The much-touted steel gardenia.” He nuzzled the palm of her hand with his chin. “I’m quaking in my boots.”

“As you should.” She cut her eyes at him. “Tell me why this would have been a perfect place for you and Cotton.”

His eyes returned to the farm acreage. “Not only for me. A great place for foster siblings to reunite for a short time. A week. If I had a million dollars…”

“What would you do?”

He tried to shrug off her question. “Doesn’t matter.”

“It matters to me.” She elbowed him in the ribs.

“Ow…”

“Start talking, cowboy. Doesn’t cost anything to dream. I want to hear what cowboy Coasties dream about?”

His heart thudded. This cowboy Coastie dreamed of Beatrice Elizabeth Duer forever in his arms. But that he couldn’t share. So he settled for a safer, as impractical, impossibility.

“Over there,” He gestured at the treelined ridge. “I’d build cabins to house the boys and girls.”

She nodded. “A foster kids camp. Bunk beds. I’m envisioning horse and nautical motifs.”

"No surprise, Girly-Girl, you'd seize on the decorative portions of the dream first."

"We use the gifts we're given, Coastie." She lifted one shoulder and let it drop. "What else is in this foster camp vision of yours?"

"I'd assign each sibling their own personal horse for the week. And bonding time activities with the brothers or sisters they only get to visit once or twice a year, if ever."

She smiled. "Learning much more than how to ride and care for an animal. Learning trust, empathy, teamwork and life skills."

Brow creasing, he stared at her. She'd managed to totally grasp his hitherto unvoiced, secret dream.

Honey motioned toward the inlet. "And water sports. Fishing. Canoeing. Clamming. Marsh muck. 'Cause this would be a Shore thing."

Sawyer moistened his lips. "The sky's the limit in our pretend world."

Honey released a gust of air. "I like our pretend world."

So did he.

He forced himself to look away from her rapt expression. "We better get going. I've got to feed the horses, and there was that problem at the lodge you wanted me to fix."

She sighed. Relief or resignation? If he died right now on a horse overlooking the water with Honey in his arms, he'd die forever happy and blessed.

With reluctance, he turned the mare toward the barn.

He—and Honey—went stall to stall feeding the horses. She, of course, fed them with typical Honey flair. Clad once again in those ridiculous heels.

Sawyer ran his hand over the palomino's broad back. It'd been a long while since he'd spent this much time with horses. "Mr. Keller comes home from rehab tomorrow. Guess my work here is about done."

"And you've loved every minute of it, haven't you?"

He raised his eyes to find Honey studying him, a pucker between those perfectly plucked brows. A rightness settled in his heart. Despite their teasing of each other, she always seemed to know him best. Better sometimes than he understood himself.

"Yeah. I have."

She hung over the stall door, watching him groom Froggy. It wasn't too hard to imagine her as a child—a little girl who didn't like to get her clothes dirty. But who, once provoked, could give as good as she got.

And he would've been the self-appointed one messing with her hair, chasing her with a reptile, pushing her into the mud… He felt a great deal of kinship with Max these days.

"Whatcha thinking about?"

He ducked his head. "Nothing. Ready to go?" He swung the door—and Honey—wide.

Light-footed, she leaped to the ground. Wobbled in her heels. "I'm ready when you are."

Sawyer doubted that very much. He followed her in his Chevy out to the Duer Lodge. She waited for him at the bottom of the wide-planked porch steps.

His breath hitched when he beheld the gaping holes like missing teeth in the railing. Three spindles lay on the ground between the dwarf gardenia bushes. "What happened here?"

Climbing the steps, he examined the damage to the railing. "Looks like someone took a…" He glanced at Honey.

Refusing to meet his gaze, she stared off into the distance, twirling a strand of hair around her finger. A sneaking suspicion grew in his mind.

Sawyer reclined against one of the pillars and rested one booted foot over his ankle. "Vandals, you say?"

Her eyes flitted to his. "Vandals." Her gaze darted away again. "Think you can fix it?"

"I'm gonna try."

"Good. Thank you." Her mouth softened. "Are you available to paint tomorrow? I can't trust anyone else to do as good a job as you."

Sawyer tilted his head. "Thought you couldn't wait to be rid of me, Beatrice, once the job was done?"

Honey leaned against another porch pillar and folded her arms across her jacket. "Exactly. We're not finished yet. Not by a long shot."

Sawyer's heart pounded at the look on her face. If only…

Her eyes beckoned. "Also… I owe you a date."

Sawyer pushed off from the column. "You don't owe—"

"Yes, I do." She raised her chin. "That was our agreement regarding whoever had the best rubber duck finish. I keep my side of a bargain."

Cold turkey was appearing less and less palatable. Time enough to nurse his broken heart once he transferred to Station Emerald Isle. "How about Tuesday night?"

She stuck out her hand. "Deal."

He clasped her hand. Goose bumps skittered across his arms. "Deal."

Sawyer glanced around the wraparound porch. "And Beatrice? You might want to keep a better watch out for those vandals so nothing else gets damaged."

That earned him a smile. The sweet, flirty Honey smile he remembered from three years ago.

"No worries." She waved her hand. "I know where to go when I need something fixed."

His stomach did that curious clutching, clenching thing it did whenever she was around. He'd look forward to their coming date with equal amounts of dread and anticipation. What was he doing—going on a date with Honey? What was the point in pursuing a relationship with someone like her?

Main thing that needed fixing was his head for torturing himself with what could never be.

Because his heart, Sawyer had figured out a long time ago, was beyond fixing when it came to Honey Duer.

Chapter Seventeen

"Talk about cutting it close, baby sis? I thought I'd have to pry you away from the inn with a crowbar."

Honey made a face in the dresser mirror. "I know how to use one of those now, you know."

Amelia smirked. "Thanks to Sawyer. Whom you're going to keep waiting if you don't finish getting ready. Dad promised the punch list would be completed without your supervision."

"But I didn't get to unwrap the plastic from the mantel Dad installed this afternoon."

"No need to micromanage every detail. Dad can handle it. You'll see the finished product soon enough."

Honey concentrated on applying the plum-toned gloss to her lips. She frowned at her shaking hand.

Amelia laughed, not missing Honey's unsteadiness. "The anticipation mounts, eh Honey?"

"It's not like we haven't been out before."

Amelia feathered a tendril of hair over Honey's shoulder. "But it's the first in a long time. And the night is young. Full of possibilities."

Honey sank onto the bed. "New beginnings."

She could hardly wait to be back in her attic bedroom.

"Seems like not too long ago we were getting you all gussied up for the big Coastie ball with Braeden."

"And it was you who helped me figure out what I really wanted." Amelia tucked the lacy shawl around Honey's shoulders. "Now I'm an old married woman with two fabulous children."

"If only I knew what to do about Sawyer and me."

Amelia eased down beside her. "I think you're overthinking things. You love him and he—"

"Stop right there." Honey held up her hand, palm out. "I never said I loved him. And who knows what the ever stoic Sawyer Kole thinks or feels."

Her sister rolled her eyes. "Denial doesn't become you, Honey. It's obvious he's crazy about you. He asked you out, didn't he?"

Actually, the date—as Honey recollected—involved her asking him. And with some arm twisting, he'd agreed as if against his better judgment.

"Sawyer's more than proven his sincerity and trustworthiness." Amelia waved her hand. "Just look at the hours he's devoted to restoring the lodge." She cocked her hand. "And not because he loves the smell of wood chips and paint."

Honey glanced toward the window overlooking Mrs. Crockett's driveway. The furniture had gone into the house this afternoon, thanks to neighbors and off duty Coasties. But Dad had insisted they wait to move in tomorrow, allowing any lingering traces of paint fumes to dissipate before bringing Baby Patrick and Max into the house.

The lodge would reopen to guests next weekend in time for Harbor Fest. And none of it would have been possible without Sawyer. So why couldn't she bring herself to admit those three little words? Why still so reluctant to trust?

"What are you afraid of, Honey?"

Her mouth trembled. "I'm scared of loving and being

let down again. Scared of giving my heart and soul only to be abandoned again."

"Your soul belongs to God, Honey. Once you make that right, I think everything else will fall into place. Because if you're honest, your heart has never stopped belonging to Sawyer Kole."

She made a face. "Love is so messy."

Amelia laughed. "So beyond your micromanaging control."

Honey sighed. "Exactly."

"And so wondrously, marvelously beyond your greatest imagining. Same as with God, if you have the courage to believe and step out in faith."

Honey spun the pearl stud on her earlobe. "Where I can free-fall onto the rocks below."

"Where always the loving arms of God await, no matter what."

"Trusting Sawyer is one thing." Honey shook her head. "I'm not sure I'm ready to trust God, too. Not after what happened to Mom and Lindi."

Her sister's eyes softened. "Truth is, I'm afraid you may not be able to have one without the other. Not if you seek real peace and happiness. But only you can make that decision to open your heart to Sawyer and God."

At the sound of tires crunching on the oyster shell driveway, Honey glanced out the window. "He's here. Maybe after Harbor Fest I'll have the time for a new beginning with Sawyer and God. Better to take things slow."

"Don't leave things too late, Honey. Life rarely goes as we plan. And if we've learned anything from Mom and Lindi's deaths, it's best not to put off what should be done or said today. I've always wondered if we'd said or done something, tried harder with Caroline..." Amelia steered Honey toward the stairs. "A topic best saved for another day. Off you go, time for your new beginning."

Honey found Sawyer waiting downstairs in the foyer. He and her dad had their heads close together, whispering. Sawyer's eyes warmed when she appeared on the landing.

The Coastie didn't look too shabby, either, in his fitted jeans. And underneath his blazer, the indigo blue dress shirt heightened the contrast with his light blue eyes and wind-bronzed tan. Being Sawyer, the shirt remained untucked as usual during his off duty hours.

He held out his hand. She curled her fingers around his. His eyes sparkled at her. "You look…"

"Yep, she does." Her dad clapped a hand on each of their shoulders, shoving them toward the door. "Don't you two have somewhere to be? Daylight's not the only thing burning." He scratched the side of his neck and darted his eyes at Sawyer. "If you get my drift."

She flicked a look in her father's direction. Three years ago he'd have met Sawyer on the porch with a shotgun. My, how times had changed.

"Yessir. You're right." Sawyer ushered her out the door and toward his truck.

Her heart drummed with anticipation. Maybe it was time to jump. And to learn to fly.

She looked so good in the silky, black sheath dress. So elegant with her hair waving around her shoulders. The ubiquitous pearls at her earlobes and around her throat. The strappy black sandals on her slim, arched feet. Too good to be sitting in his old pickup truck. Too good for him, the throwaway kid from Oklahoma.

His heart sank. She deserved so much more than what he had to offer. Seeing her tonight made his decision clearer and yet harder at the same time.

The silence between them lengthened as he kept the headlights pointed toward Kiptohanock.

She cleared her throat. "I didn't see you earlier at the inn. You must have been busy today."

He wound his hands tighter around the steering wheel. "You're seeing me now."

She smiled. "You're right. Where are we going?"

He kept his eyes fastened on the asphalt, the lights bouncing off one side of the forested Seaside Road to the other. "It's a surprise. You don't have to know everything. Relax."

"That's asking a lot from a control freak like me." She slid across the seat, her hip touching his. "Will I like the surprise?"

His lips curved at the tremulous little girl sound in her voice. The nearness of the grown-up Honey, however, did funny things to his nerve endings. "I think you will. I *hope* you will."

Turning into the Duer drive, he heard her breath catch. Her face transformed at the sight of the string of lights dotting the wraparound porch. The house glowed in the blue velvet dusk of the Eastern Shore twilight. Bell-shaped lanterns lit the oyster shell path from the driveway to the front steps.

"When did—? How?" She touched her hand to her throat. "You and Dad."

"This afternoon." Seeing the rapt look on her face, Sawyer swallowed hard. It meant everything giving Honey her dream. "No easy feat keeping you away from here long enough to install everything."

"Your dad insisted he'd complete the finishing touches so I could go to Keller's and shower—lucky for you. Seth arrived at Mrs. Crockett's only seconds before me. You're not an easy girl to surprise, Beatrice. Did we?" Sawyer cut his eyes at her, unnerved by her silence. "Surprise you?"

Her eyes welled. "Oh, yes. You're full of surprises."

"Well, come on then." He threw open the truck door. "The real surprise is inside."

Instead of waiting for him to come round to the passenger side, she scooted out behind him. Enjoying her anticipation, he drew her to the porch. With a dramatic flourish, he threw open the refurbished oak door and thoroughly delighted in her gasp of pleasure.

"Oh, Sawyer." She hurried inside. "It's like a Currier and Ives lithograph. Thank you."

Per Sawyer's exact instructions, Seth had done him proud. Dozens of candles were scattered across every available surface in the great room. The votives lent an old-fashioned warmth, luminescent in hurricane globes.

She flitted from one side of the room to the other. His hands stuffed in his pockets, Sawyer remained in the doorway, letting her make her own discoveries. Enjoying her exploration of her restored family home.

The sea glass and driftwood decor she'd collected over the years from the barrier islands once more adorned the Queen Anne table in front of the bay window. Seth's checkerboard crowned the piecrust table. She ran a loving hand over the knotted pine beadboard walls.

"I can't believe you were able to..." She caught sight of the mantel. "Oh, Sawyer. What did you do?" Two tears rolled down her cheeks.

"Hey, now." He moved forward. "No tears. This is supposed to be a happy occasion."

"This *is* me happy." On her tiptoes, she threw her arms around him.

Grunting at the force of her embrace, he staggered, but his arms tightened around her. "If this is happy, I'd hate to see you unhappy," he whispered into the gardenia fragrance of her hair brushing his cheek.

She grabbed his hand and tugged him toward the fireplace. She scanned the Duer family portrait remounted above the mantel. Taken, she'd told him once, when everything and everyone had been safe in her childhood world.

"Before Caroline went away," Honey whispered as if to herself. "Before the cancer took Mom and Daddy fell into the darkness. Before Lindi..."

Sawyer, however, couldn't tear his eyes away from Honey. And he thought his heart might burst from loving her. If nothing else, he'd managed to do this one thing right. To give Honey back her home and, in a small way, her family.

Her eyes fell to the mantel. She let go of his hand and trailed her fingers along the grooves he'd etched into the wood. "How did you manage to find the exact—?" She swung around. "There's no way you could buy an exact replica of a nineteenth-century handcrafted mantel. You carved this yourself, didn't you?"

Once again, she threw her arms around him, almost knocking Sawyer off his feet. "When did you sleep? No wonder you fell asleep every time you got still. How did you manage to hide this until now? Oh, Sawyer..."

He grinned into her hair. "I repeat, you're not an easy person to surprise, Beatrice. Always got to have your nose in everybody's business."

She pulled back a few inches and play-slapped his arm. "Keller's barn loft. That's why you went all funny when I showed up there. You're something else, you know that? Something else."

He examined her face. "Something good? Or something bad?"

She fingered the ditch daisy lying between the hurricane lamps at either end of the mantel. "I...I..." She stopped smiling.

His heart lurched.

Uncertainty clouded her features. She searched his face for assurances he couldn't give her. "Maybe we—"

"We'll always be friends."

Her eyes glistened. "Right." She glanced away. "The best kind of friends," she whispered.

Friends… Not what he longed for. More than he deserved.

If he had any sense at all, he'd walk her out to the truck, forego what he'd planned and drive her back to her family. But Sawyer had never possessed much good sense when it came to Honey Duer. Tonight had the potential to break his heart even further.

Yet he couldn't leave things as they were between them. As they should be between them. Not without once… Just one more time…

Because tonight… Sawyer had only tonight. And God help him, tonight needed to be enough to last him a lifetime.

He moved toward the heirloom Victrola and cranked it. He winced as the scratchy melody from before the First World War floated to the eaves of the high-ceilinged room. Her eyes widened.

"Let Me Call You Sweetheart" seemed presumptuous at this point. But he'd spoken truly when he'd told her a few weeks ago he'd take what he could get. She was right about him.

He was a self-admitted adrenaline junkie, a man of action. Uncomfortable with words. He'd chosen this song once Seth showed him the box of 78s. Chosen this song to express what he himself could not.

And facing long weeks of loneliness ahead, he wanted to always remember her as she was now in the glow of the candlelight, her face shining.

"I made you a promise and I keep my promises." He took a deep breath. "Dance with me, Beatrice?"

She twisted the pearls at her throat.

"One dance." He swallowed. "Before I ship out next week."

"You're leaving next week?" she whispered.

"Station Emerald Isle."

What was glaringly obvious to Honey at this moment was that he'd only asked her to dance. Not go with him.

She couldn't deny the truth of her feelings for him any longer. Her gaze landed on the flower. She muffled the tiny sob that rose in her throat. Sawyer knew her in the deep places she barely admitted to herself.

Why hadn't she told him how she felt? But something—pride?—held her back. She'd been about to tell him, but fear got the best of her.

He'd never said he loved her. Never told her the things she longed to hear from him. Was everything he'd done for her over the past few months merely him keeping a promise or making amends?

Pain sliced through Honey. Why didn't Sawyer tell her what was in his heart? Perhaps, though, he *was* telling her. In his own way, he was telling her good-bye.

Sawyer held out his hand. Conflicting emotions rippled across his face. Sadness. Joy. A fierce vulnerability. His gaze traveled to her mouth. And lingered.

Her heart beating faster than the 3/4 time of the waltz, she took his hand. Her eyes locked onto his. And his eyes went opaque, a smoky blue.

With her hand clasped in his and his other arm around her waist, Sawyer maintained a careful distance between their bodies. She placed her free hand on the broad length of his shoulder.

Elbow up and carriage erect, he never took his eyes off her face. His hold never wavered as he led Honey in the waltz.

Let me call you sweetheart, I'm in love with you, warbled a long-dead singer.

A muscle ticked in his cheek. Sawyer tightened his jaw.

Let me hear you whisper that you love me, too...

The music and the words flowed over her like gentle rain.

Keep the love light glowing in your eyes so true—

His chest rose and fell as if he were having difficulty drawing breath.

Let me call you sweetheart, I'm in love with you.

The music faded. The singer's voice died away. But Sawyer didn't let go. As if as reluctant as she for this dance to end. For their time to end.

Round and round the turntable, the needle scratched.

And then Sawyer stopped.

Sawyer removed his arm from her waist. It took him longer to relinquish her hand. "Thank you, Beatrice." He stepped back.

Her heart pounded. "Must we stop?" Her words were fraught with more than she dared ask.

Sawyer moved away and lifted the needle from the gramophone. Going from candle to candle, he extinguished the light. "It's for the best."

"Best for whom?"

He paused, his hand cupped around the rim of the hurricane globe. "Best for you."

She seized the flower wilting on the mantel. "Stop assuming you know what's best for me."

He straightened. Only the moonlight broke the darkness of the room. His eyes flicked over her face. "Time to go to dinner."

"I'm suddenly not hungry."

Sawyer held out his hand. "Then I'll take you home."

Honey lifted her chin. "I thought that's where we were."

Sawyer's mouth quivered before he gained mastery over

it. "A guy like me doesn't have a home, Beatrice. You ought to know that about me by now."

He dropped his hand. "Can we just go now…please?"

Without another word, she shouldered past him out onto the porch. As she waited for him to secure the door, she wanted to weep. For herself. For him.

But most of all, for them. For who they could've been together.

Chapter Eighteen

Sector Hampton Roads radioed the Station Kiptohanock watchstander the following afternoon. A few miles offshore one of the barrier islands, an engine room fire had erupted onboard a cargo ship. The watch duty crew headed for the fast boat tied to the station dock. Sawyer was halfway out the door when Braeden stopped him.

"Do not under any circumstances set foot on that vessel, XPO."

"But twelve souls are listed on the crew list." Sawyer scanned the information sheet he'd been handed. "The *Cartagena* is carrying almost 20,000 tons of flammable chemicals. Mainly methyl tertiary..." Sawyer squinted at the words. "Butyl ether and iso...buta...nol."

Braeden crossed his arms over his chest. "We don't have the proper protective gear, nor do you have the training to deal with that kind of 'tetra-methyl-kill-you' cargo, Sawyer."

"Chief—"

Braeden's jaw tightened. "The Atlantic Strike Team helo out of Elizabeth City will be en route to the burning ship. Fires are what they do. They've got the specialized equipment and training. Let the AST do what they do best."

Sawyer bristled. “We’ve got the makings of an ecological disaster. Suppose—”

“With that type of cargo, if you set one foot on that tanker you’ll be court-martialed per regulation.” Braeden jabbed a finger in Sawyer’s chest. “You just need to do your job. And your job is to bring the crew—the tanker’s and ours—back to Kiptohanock.”

Sawyer scowled.

Braeden got in his face. “You roger that, Petty Officer Kole?”

Sawyer went into a rigid salute, feet clamped together. “Roger that, Chief.”

On board the response boat, Sawyer shouldered aside the bos’n mate and took the wheel himself. He needed to do something with his hands. Anything to keep his mind busy.

It’d been a restless night, replaying the image of Honey’s face over and over again in his head. In two days, Kiptohanock would celebrate Harbor Fest. In four, he’d be pointing the nose of his truck toward Highway 13, the Bay Bridge Tunnel and the Outer Banks of North Carolina.

Sawyer maneuvered past the other watercraft bobbing in the harbor until he cleared the marina. Shifting into higher gear, he spared one last look over his shoulder at the shoreline where the white steeple of the church pierced the azure blue of the November sky.

Going full throttle in the inlet, he steered the boat past the barrier islands and out toward the open sea. When he gunned it, Wiggins grinned at Sawyer and widened his stance to accommodate the roll and swell of the waves.

His heart heavy, Sawyer nonetheless smiled in return. “You know the only difference between a buccaneer and a Coastie, BMC First Class Wiggins?” he repeated in an echo of Braeden Scott’s words to him once upon a time.

Wiggins’s brow furrowed. “No, Boats, I don’t. What *is* the difference between buccaneers and Coasties?”

Sawyer's lips curved into a smile. Boats—the Coastie term of affection for boat-driving guardsmen.

"Nothing, Wiggins." He inhaled a hearty draught of sea air. "There is no difference at all between a buccaneer and a Coastie."

Wiggins's chest rumbled. The other guardsmen barked with laughter.

Sawyer's shoulders lifted and fell. "Old joke, Coasties. An old joke."

The laughter died when they spotted the cargo ship. Crew members waved from the tilted deck. None of them wore lifejackets. Several of the men's faces were burned.

Listing starboard, the stern lay submerged in water. Smoke billowed from below deck. Flames licked midship. Gusty winds and choppy waves rocked the tanker, hampering Sawyer's effort to bring the response boat alongside.

"We've got to transfer those men off the ship." Sawyer edged the boat as close as he dared and cut back the engine. "But one spark and we could be blown to kingdom come."

Seaman Apprentice Marshall nodded. "Watchstander reports the Strike Team's inbound, XPO."

"Affirmative." Sawyer glanced around at the men and women. "Now, let's do *our* thing."

His crew knew their jobs. Handing the controls over to the bosun's mate, Sawyer helped transfer the men off the tanker's deck to the fast boat. Utilizing the Spanish he'd learned with the Latin American task force, he quickly ascertained all crew members were present and accounted for. Except the captain.

The first mate's eyes darted toward the bulkheads. The crew had managed to seal the containers in number three and four holds, he told Sawyer. They'd attempted to smother the blaze with carbon dioxide. But the captain remained behind to seal off the most combustive of the containers in hold five.

Sawyer imagined the barrier islands and the wildlife coated in petroleum and worse. He envisioned the leaking chemicals ebbing toward Kiptohanock, destroying the seaside beauty of the Eastern Shore and killing its marine life. He grimaced, helpless to prevent the larger tragedy.

The captain lurched onto the main deck. The deck roiled beneath his feet. A ripple effect brought the response boat within inches of the cargo ship. There was a collective gasp from the tanker's shivering crew. The bosun's mate barely managed to avoid colliding into the side of the burning tanker and into disaster.

"The captain's going to have to jump for it." Sawyer exchanged a glance with Wiggins. "Then you get us away from this ship ASAP."

"We're too far for him to make it. I can't get the boat any closer, XPO, not in these conditions."

Sawyer took stock of the worsening weather. "Steady as she goes, BMC. Try to maintain a distance of at least two or three feet. Hold her as steady as you can for as long as you can."

"Affirmative."

Sawyer bellowed through the horn and explained to the captain what needed to happen next.

But resisting Sawyer's attempts to hurry him off the sinking vessel, the captain warned in broken English of fire and of the chemical cargo that must be secured.

Waiting on the rail, the CG crew members urged the man to jump. Sawyer kept an eye on the timing of the swells. *"Uno..."* he yelled. He held up his hand and ticked off his fingers for the captain's benefit. *"Dos..."*

The tanker shuddered. The panicked captain didn't wait for the count to reach three. He leaped. With a splash, the captain went into the water. He disappeared from sight.

"Where is he?" Marshall shouted. "I can't find him."

Life ring ready to throw, Perez paced the deck. "Keep looking."

"How long can we search, XPO?" Wiggins gripped the wheel. "The ship's going to blow any moment."

Sawyer kept his eyes trained on the spot where he'd last seen the captain. "Take the boat out of harm's way, Wiggins. I'm not giving up on him."

"With all due respect—"

"That's an order, BMC. Do it now."

Sawyer dived over the side. He plunged beneath the swells and swam the distance separating him from the captain's last location. But when he came up for air, he found no one. The oily film on the water stung his eyes. He swiped his hand across his burning eyes.

Then from the interior of the ship came a deafening boom. The echoing shock wave resounded across the water. Sawyer jolted. Searing heat blasted his face.

Flinching, he ducked as the detonation spewed jagged shards of twisted metal. Underwater, he dodged the flying debris and waited for the fiery hailstorm to abate. Below, he watched in horror as the red hot fragments ignited the water around him. He scanned the surface above for an open space in which to emerge. A place free of the flames. A place where he could find breathable oxygen. He couldn't wait much longer…

Rocketing upward, his body shot out of the water, his lungs heaving. Coughing and hacking the vile brew out of his lungs, he erupted into a world aflame. Fire engulfed the water around him in all directions.

Scissoring, he dove again. The circle of fire tightened like a noose in his wake. But there was nowhere left to return to.

And he knew in that instant he'd never make it. Time was up. No more second chances.

It seemed to him he'd been fighting, one way or the other, to survive his whole life. And he was tired. So tired.

Sawyer couldn't hold his breath forever. He could choose to drown. Or to burn.

He prayed Wiggins had gotten the boat away in time. And in that instant, Sawyer was overwhelmed with gratitude for being reassigned to Kiptohanock. For one last opportunity to make things right. Despite his best efforts, bubbles of oxygen escaped his mouth and nostrils.

Sawyer's chest deflated. He was losing oxygen too rapidly. He squeezed his eyes shut.

In his memories, he experienced again the eight-second thrill of riding an equine tornado. He felt once more the spray of the surf on his face. He beheld from long ago, his five-year-old sister torn out of his arms. He basked in the pride he felt every time he donned the Coastie blue uniform.

He envisioned the Duer home glowing with light. The sound of an old-fashioned melody. The white steeple piercing the sky above Kiptohanock.

Something exploded somewhere close by. Churning the water—along with Sawyer—like the wringer on a washing machine. And his last coherent thought?

Of brown-eyed Susans.

Chapter Nineteen

After a sleepless night, she'd gotten a late start on the move-in. One of those days when nothing seemed to go right. Honey grimaced. Make that a lifetime of nothing going right.

Her sister and Baby Patrick left for an infant well-visit. Honey ended up taking Max to school. Before she knew it, half the day had gotten away from her, and it was afternoon before she managed to shake her lethargy, gather some boxes and head to the inn.

But the real reason it took her so long to get moving? It took her that long to summon the courage to return to the inn and face how, once again, Sawyer Kole had torn her heart in two.

With enormous dread, she drove alone to the house. Unlocking the door, she heaved her suitcase over the threshold. She ignored with a fierce determination the doused candles and silent phonograph. She headed straight for her bedroom to unpack.

It was the bell she heard first.

The sound of the bell rang over the trees. Above the rooftop. Over the watery expanse separating the inn from the village.

Stuffing her folded jeans into a drawer, she paused and

lifted her head. Across the marsh, a flock of startled birds rose, cawing.

Honey cocked her ear toward the window. There it was again. The bell. Tolling as relentless as the tide.

She shivered. A cold metallic sound. Dull as impending death. Her bones vibrated with each clamor of the bell. Clanging across each tidal creek the bell rang, summoning Kiptohanock residents in situations of extreme maritime disaster.

Honey's breath caught. Never in her lifetime had the bell rung, except for the annual blessing of the fleet. Dad still talked about the nor'easter that crushed a half-dozen fishing boats when he was a boy, and how the bell had tolled then.

She covered her hands over her ears. *No, God. No more.*

Her first thought was of her dad out on a charter. And then her mind jerked to Sawyer. Because whatever had happened, she knew as sure as she knew Sawyer he'd be in the thick of it. That's who he was. More than likely, both he and Braeden.

She raced out of the attic, down the stairs and out the front door toward her dad's truck. Cranking the engine, she hit the accelerator. Oyster shells spitting beneath her spinning tires, she hurtled out of the driveway and toward Kiptohanock.

In the village, a crowd lined the seawall, the wharf and the Sandpiper Cafe parking lot. The red-and-white lights of three ambulances whirred. The paramedics waited on the Coast Guard dock with multiple gurneys.

Not a good sign. What had happened? Who was hurt? And despite the crowd, an eerie silence hung over the waterfront, broken only by the sharp cries of the seagulls swooping above the harbor.

In the distance, a Coast Guard response boat approached. Circling the square, she slipped into one of the last remaining parking spots near the church. She vaulted out of the truck and plowed her way through the bystanders to the outer edge of the adjacent town pier. She spotted a tight-lipped Braeden catch the rope a guardsmen threw from the fast boat chugging into the station dock.

Relief for Amelia and Max flooded her heart. But what about her dad? Her gaze ran over the people pressing at her back and out toward the fishing boats moored in the marina. There, tied at another slip, the *Now I Sea.*

Her father—Honey's head swiveled—he had to be somewhere close. But where was Sawyer? She scanned the guardsmen emptying out of the rescue boat.

Paramedics rushed forward as one by one the guardsmen staggered onto the dock, their arms slung across the shoulders of the foreign nationals they'd rescued. Both the American and foreign-born seamen sported an assortment of burns and wounds.

Honey took a mental count. Marshall. Endicott. Perez. Schilling. Braeden took hold of Wiggins. Her heart pounded at the utter grief etched on the bosun mate's face.

Shaking his head, words poured out of the young man's mouth. The words floated across the water. Natural disaster. Explosion. Flying shrapnel. Couldn't get to him.

Her heart skipped a beat. Her eyes searched the now empty fast boat. Where was Sawyer?

"Come on," she muttered under her breath. "Let me see that blond towhead of yours."

Wiggins sagged, and Braeden transferred him to the care of a paramedic. Braeden caught her eye across the channel. He shook his head at someone behind her.

"No." Honey fisted her hands. "No." Someone touched her shoulder.

"Honey…" As if in a dream—a nightmare—the gravelly voice of her father. "Wiggins radioed the station as soon as he could."

She flung off his hand. “It isn’t true.” Her gaze searched the horizon.

Her father launched into a brief summary of the events of a SAR gone wrong.

“Why did they leave him? He’s out there, Daddy.”

Her father closed his eyes momentarily. “The boat was caught in the explosion, too. There were injuries. Wiggins did the right thing. He had to get those men medical attention. But the cargo ship—there’s a huge debris field, Honey.”

She jabbed her finger toward the open sea beyond the barrier islands. “They need to get back out there and find him.”

Her dad took hold of her arm. “The Hercs from Air Station Elizabeth City are on scene now. The ROMEO fishing fleet, we’re headed out, too, to help with the recovery. But Honey, it will be getting dark soon…”

She wrenched free of his grasp. “Recovery? What happened to rescue? He’s not—” Honey strove to contain the rising note of hysteria in her voice. “It can’t end this way. Not like this.”

“Braeden says we can wait inside the station for updates.” At her elbow, tears coursed across Amelia’s face.

She’d not noticed her sister’s arrival. Honey shook her head. “No,” she whispered.

“The Guard is doing everything they can, Honey. But—”

“I won’t believe it. Not until I see him.”

Amelia’s mouth quivered. “Honey, you grew up here. You know sometimes they never find—”

“Stop it!” Honey yanked free of their restraining hands. She shouldered through the silent bystanders, past her friends, past the men and women she’d known her entire life.

“Honey…” her dad cried.

"Let her go," Amelia called. "She needs to come to terms with this in her own way."

Unable to bear the sympathy in their eyes, she stumbled past the diner. Somehow without realizing it, Honey found herself on the lawn of the church.

Her gaze shot to the white steeple Sawyer had almost broken his neck to restore. And a seething rage—the anger she'd kept stuffed inside herself since she was a girl—rose, lava-hot, to the surface. Foaming. Out of control.

"Why, Sawyer?" she screamed at the steeple. "Why do you always have to be the hero? Why do you take such chances?"

She shook her fist at the steeple. "And this time, you lost. What about the people you leave behind? The people whose lives will be devastated because you're not here."

"People whose lives you will ruin," she whispered.

But she knew why. He risked his life because he did care. Because he was a hero. It was who Sawyer was. What she loved the most about him.

And what she'd feared most about him.

She marched up the steps of the church and flung open the doors, which were never locked in peaceful Kiptohanock. She stalked down the aisle toward the altar. Head tilted back, she glared at the wooden cross on the altar table.

"Why did You let this happen to him? After what he went through as a boy, didn't he deserve to live to be an old, old man?"

She blinked rapidly. "Why do You hate Sawyer?" Her voice broke. "Why do You hate me?"

Only silence answered her.

She sank to her knees beside the front pew in the century-old church. And resting her head against the armrest, her body shook with sobs. Over the loss of her mom. Lindi and Caroline. For what she'd neglected to say to Sawyer.

"I love you." Her lips grazed the wood. "I love you…" Arms wrapped around herself, she rocked back and forth on the floor. "I love you."

Too little, too late. She'd never know if she'd spoken those words to him last night whether it might have altered the choices he'd made today. An image of him floating face down in the water filled her mind.

Honey moaned. She'd lost him for good this time. Like she'd lost everyone she ever loved. And she was so tired. So tired of trying to be perfect. Of maintaining this untouchable, always-got-it-together persona she'd created.

She wasn't perfect. Perfection was an illusion of control. Only God was perfect. Somewhere along the way she'd turned away from Him because He didn't do things her way. Condemnation for the choices she'd made flooded Honey. Condemnation—something Sawyer had struggled with until he found—

Honey opened her eyes. A black Bible nestled against the corner of the cushion. An old bulletin stuck into its contents piqued her curiosity. Romans, he'd said.

She pried the Bible loose. Her knees scraping the hard wooden floor, she held her breath and opened the book to its bookmarked position. And her eyes widened. What were the chances…?

There is now no condemnation for those who are in Christ Jesus.—Romans 8

The "in Christ Jesus" part was key. Like for her mom and Lindi. Despite sickness and mistakes.

Another highlighted section toward the end of the chapter snagged Honey's attention.

What then shall we say to these things?... God did not spare His own Son...

Her eyes drifted toward the cross on the altar. Her gaze dropped to the printed page.

Who shall separate us from the love of Christ? Shall

tribulation, or distress, or persecution, or famine, or nakedness, or danger, or sword?

She understood about separation. First, her mom. Then, Lindi. Caroline's inexplicable desertion. Sawyer. One after the other, she'd lost them.

But had she? Despite her father's encompassing grief, he'd fought his way through the darkness toward faith. As had Amelia and little Max. As had Sawyer.

Were those she loved the most gone forever?

No...

Her breath hitched as if the words written two thousand years ago had been written today, just for her. Though she'd probably skimmed these words a dozen times, they became suddenly alive with meaning.

She hungered for the peace those words had given Sawyer and her family. To know. To believe.

Her mother. Lindi. Wherever Caroline and Sawyer even now found themselves. They weren't lost to her forever. Not gone. Because of God's love for them and for Honey, too—they were okay. Better than okay. Just okay somewhere else.

"Forgive me." She bowed her head. "Help me to trust You."

She knelt in a pool of sunlight at the foot of the cross. Bathed in the rainbow squares of stained glass that dappled the altar. And she knew, whatever the search revealed, she'd be okay, too.

Never alone or forsaken. Forever safe in the loving arms of God. Like her mom and Lindi.

Like Sawyer?

"Please keep him alive," she breathed. "Please bring him back to me."

In the end, though, everything always came back to trust. Faith. And surrender.

"But Your will..." Her mouth trembled. "Not mine, be done."

Chapter Twenty

As the fiery sunset faded to dusk, her sister found Honey in front of the altar.

"Where are Baby Patrick and Max?" Honey whispered.

Amelia hugged Honey. "With Miss Pauline."

Darkness descended across Kiptohanock. Reverend Parks arrived and lit the candles on the altar. She winced as the light from the tapers flickered across the sea blue walls of the sanctuary. Because she remembered other candles. Another night. Last night.

The reverend was joined by his wife, the Sandpiper Cafe owner and Honey's waitress friend, Dixie. Others, too, like Mrs. Francis, the troop leader. The town postmistress. The soon-to-retire librarian, Mrs. Beal. And Mr. Keller, newly released from rehab.

Praying. Singing hymns. Comforting each other.

It was the way of the Kiptohanock faithful. Humbled, she was struck with how much larger her true family was, more than she'd imagined. And she was grateful.

But the hours ticked by with no word of Sawyer. She breathed in the scent of wax and the leather of the Bible she'd clutched to her chest during the long night. The candles burned low on the altar.

Yet as the darkness of the night surrendered to the first streaks of dawn, she heard the bell.

Slumped against the side of a pew, Honey jolted. Amelia seized her hand. Heads turned.

Throwing off Amelia's arm, she staggered to her feet. Squinting at the glare of the sunrise, she dashed out of the church. Behind her, a steady stream of prayer warriors followed close on her heels.

One of her dad's ROMEO friends rocked the mounted bell from side to side. The clapper clanged against the metal. Catching sight of Honey, Seaman Apprentice Reaves on the adjacent dock gestured toward the open channel.

Where a small flotilla of vessels—Coast Guard, fishing and recreational—chugged into the harbor. Honey identified Braeden at the helm of a response boat. Her dad manned the wheel of the *Now I Sea*.

Please... Please bring Sawyer back... Please.

She raced toward the Coast Guard dock. She stopped a few yards away, her eyes floating toward the morning sky. Red sky last night, sailor's delight.

Let him be okay...

And if he wasn't? She lifted her face toward the steeple. Either way, in the end, they'd both be okay.

Wiggins, a bandage swathing his forehead, leaped to catch the mooring line Dawkins tossed. Braeden cut the engine. The station-side Coasties went into action. Honey strained on her tiptoes to see, but their height blocked her view of the interior of the boat.

Hands knotted, she held her breath. Time went into slow motion. A surreal quality fogged her vision. At the sudden caw of seagulls, her eyes shot skyward before dropping toward the end of the pier.

Then...

A straw-colored head emerged from the boat cabin. Cut high and cropped close on the sides in the Coastie buzz. Braeden's arm around him on one side. Wiggins surged forward to support him on the other side.

She dug her fingernails into her palms. Her eyes stung. She blinked the moisture away. "Sawyer!"

His head lifted. His face blackened with smoke, those sky blue eyes of his burned bright.

She ran the length of the pier. Tears rolling down her cheeks, she crossed the remaining distance separating them. He was alive. *Thank You, God.* Sawyer was alive.

Honey flung herself at him, knocking Braeden's arm from around Sawyer. The restraining hand of Wiggins on Sawyer's back only just prevented them from falling into the Kiptohanock drink.

"Whoa there," Braeden reared. "Give him a chance to—"

"Are you hurt?" She gripped Sawyer's shoulders. "I love you." She brushed a kiss across his cracked lips.

His mouth opened, but no sound emerged.

"Are you bleeding anywhere?" Her gaze flitted from the top of his wind-blown hair down his torso. "I love you." She kissed the corner of his mouth.

He stared at her.

"Is anything broken?" She scanned his torn uniform for injuries. She cupped his cheek. "I love you." She kissed him again.

His forehead creased.

"I'm so sorry, Sawyer." She smoothed his collar into place. "Will you forgive me for not telling you before how much I love you?" She plucked at his upturned sleeve, straightening it.

Sawyer's wood-roughened hands captured her restless fingers and pressed them against his chest. "Beatrice..." his voice rasped.

Her eyes flew to his. "God and I talked last night." Her mouth quivered. "And I've decided every time you say my name—" She bit her lip, working to steady her voice.

She swallowed and tried again.

"I've decided every time for the rest of your life when you say my name the right way, I'm going to kiss you."

She opened her palms flat against his uniform. His heart thrummed against her hands. A slow smile curved his lips.

Her heart pitter-pattered. As her knees threatened to give way, she was glad Sawyer had hold of her. So not fair what his smile did to her insides.

"Is that right?" His blue eyes sparked. "Beatrice isn't going to cut it anymore?"

She shook her head.

"Would you let me call you sweetheart?"

Her pulse and her heart tangoed. "That one I might take under advisement."

Sawyer brought her captured hand to his mouth and brushed his lips across her palm. "So you want me to call you Honey?"

Honey gave him a quick kiss.

Sawyer let go of her hands and wrapped his arms around her.

Honey inched back to better see his face. "You're not the only one who can keep a promise."

Sawyer's hold tightened around her waist. "I can see that." A muscle beat a furious tempo in his exposed throat. "Honey…"

Both hands gripping his collar, she kissed him once more. "I love you, Sawyer." She eased onto her heels.

His lips quirked. "Have it your own way." He cocked his head. "You always do. And I love you, too." Sawyer widened his stance. "Honey…"

Biting off a laugh, her mouth found his again. And she showed him how she intended to honor her promise. Always.

Chapter Twenty-One

"Petty Officer First Class Sawyer Ramsay Kole, do you take this woman, Beatrice Elizabeth Duer, to be your lawfully wedded wife to have and to hold from this day forward… In sickness and in health… Forsaking all others cleave only unto her… So long as you both shall live?"

At the altar of the Kiptohanock church on this glorious, if brisk, day in late November, Sawyer squeezed Honey's hand. "I do."

If Sawyer lived to be a hundred years old, he'd never forget the sight of Honey on her father's arm in a white confection of lace and satin. And the look in her eyes… Her eyes filled only with him.

Him, Sawyer Kole, the throwaway kid, one-time Oklahoma cowboy. Only worthy of this life and Honey's love because of God's mercy and grace.

And when his gaze dropped from her face to the bouquet in her hands? Sawyer thought his heart might stop. From love for this woman. For the promise in her eyes. For the joy set before them both.

She carried in her arms a bouquet of ditch flowers. Brown-eyed Susans.

Reverend Parks repeated the vows for Honey. And underneath the bouquet, Honey squeezed his fingers back. "I do."

"The ring?" Reverend Parks looked over Sawyer's shoulder. First at Max with his satin cushion of fake entwined rings tied in a nautical knot, and then at Braeden, Sawyer's best man. Envisioning rings rolling under the organ, courtesy of Max—whose true middle name was mayhem—matron of honor Amelia had insisted on Max playing a symbolic role in the nuptials.

Max cocked his head at the bridal couple and made as if to toss the pillow into the choir loft. Honey inhaled. Sawyer narrowed his eyes. With Braeden fishing the ring out of his pocket, Amelia glared and shook her head. Seth clamped a hand on Max's shoulder.

Rolling his tongue in his cheek, Max flitted his eyes toward Izzie beside her father, Weston Clark, in the front pew. Izzie stuck her tongue out at Max. And Max, with a triumphant smirk at the wedding party, lowered his arm. Slowly…

Never a dull moment with the Duer crowd. Sawyer grinned. And he wouldn't have it any other way, *thank You, God.*

The rings were exchanged. The unity candle lit. Reverend Parks prayed.

"You may kiss your bride."

With much relish, Sawyer did.

"May I present to you, Petty Officer First Class and Mrs. Sawyer Kole."

With her hand nestled into the crook of his elbow, they faced the congregation amidst much cheers and clapping.

Armistice signed. Ending the battle for Kiptohanock and Honey Duer Kole's heart for good.

They emerged from the white clapboard church between a line of Coasties, beneath a hail of flower petals to a horse and buggy Mr. Keller had loaned them for the occasion. Draped—thanks to Wiggins and company—with streamers of toilet paper. Honey's nose crinkled, but she laughed at the sight of the hand-lettered sign affixed to the rear of the buggy: My Heart Belongs to a Coastie.

Helping her inside, Sawyer bundled her skirts into the carriage, careful to keep the fabric free of the shaving cream. Entering from the other side, Sawyer gathered the reins.

Sawyer took one final look at the white steeple piercing the skyline above tiny Kiptohanock.

Slapping the reins, he clicked his tongue under his teeth, signaling the horses. Honey waved at those who'd gathered to honor them on their wedding day. Those who loved them the most. And the best. Not the least of whom God, who'd loved both Sawyer and Honey. So well and for so long.

To God, be the praise.

Did she know how to throw a party or what?

Clusters of Kiptohanockians thronged the lodge. Strings of light festooned the eaves of the house like electric gingerbread trim. Candles glowed from within. There was the sound of punch glasses clinking. Voices raised in conversation. Miss Pauline cuddled Baby Patrick. And confined to Max's bedroom upstairs, Ajax and Blackie whined, to no avail, to be let out for the fun.

From the porch, Honey peered inside the interior. In the family room, Amelia had her forearm wrapped around Max's neck. Weston Clark wrenched Izzie backward by the sash of her hunter green silk party dress.

Honey blew out a breath. She wasn't going to worry about what had gone down inside the inn. Not tonight. She'd fix whatever was damaged tomorrow. Or better yet, get Sawyer to fix it after the honeymoon.

Lips curving, her gaze wandered the length of the wrap-around porch. Surrounded by a mixed bunch of off duty Coasties and ROMEOs, her dad's arm was draped across Sawyer's shoulders. And she could tell how much her new husband basked in the blatant approval in her father's eyes. If she didn't know better, she'd swear Sawyer married her just to become the son Seth Duer never had.

She hugged herself in the chilly late autumn air as laughter erupted. Her father wound down yet another fish story. Followed by Braeden's tale of Sawyer's efforts on behalf of the captain, who'd somehow been found alive by the helo from Air Station Elizabeth City. Braeden had put Sawyer's name in consideration for a commendation.

The secondary blast had knocked Sawyer momentarily unconscious but had also propelled him free of the burning water. With his life vest keeping him afloat, Sawyer had clung to a buoyant piece of debris until the Herc spotted him floating among the wreckage. Other than a few bruised ribs and a concussion, Sawyer was okay.

She swallowed. Better than okay and thanks be to God, here with her. Honey was so blessed, and she didn't intend to waste a minute of her second chance for happiness.

She'd come out to the porch to retrieve her groom for the cutting of the nautical anchor-topped wedding cake. Honey held off for one more moment, though, enjoying Sawyer's pleasure amidst his Coastie comrades and his newfound male relations.

But with that special sixth sense he always possessed with her, Sawyer lifted his head, catching her eye. And when he looked at her like that? She sighed. Not much could beat a man in full dress blues. Especially, her man. Her heart fluttered.

He strode forward, parting the cluster of men like a

line cut through the water. Her feet went into motion of their own volition, like a fish on the other end of a hook.

Meeting at the steps, Sawyer took off his cap and placed it at a jaunty angle atop her head. The medals pressed against Honey's bare back as he engulfed her in the safe harbor of his embrace and brushed his lips against her hair.

"This shindig over yet, Honey?" he whispered. His breath blew one of the tendrils above her ear.

She kissed him.

She'd been ready to tie the matrimonial knot the day after Sawyer's rescue. Sawyer, however, was afraid she would later regret not having the wedding of her dreams. So he insisted they wait. Two weeks only, she countered, and not a day longer.

Thanks to the best bunch of girlfriends ever, Honey had the wedding of her dreams. More importantly, she had the man of her dreams. A team effort—Debbie put together the beautiful music, Miss Betty the gorgeous dress, Wanda the hair and nails, and Kathy the reception at the inn. Her good friend Cindy and Amelia made sure the little touches reflected Honey and Sawyer's joint Eastern Shore Coast Guard personalities.

Between his saved leave days, Sawyer had ample time for a honeymoon. He'd also decided not to re-up, but to finish out the last few months of his tour and return permanently to Kiptohanock to help Honey run the inn. But the lodge had stopped being Honey's priority. Sawyer was.

Station Emerald Isle would get them both—Mr. and Mrs. Sawyer Kole. Just before the wedding, however, soon-to-be new brother-in-law Senior Chief Scott sailed to the rescue. He worked it so Sawyer could put in his final months of duty at Station Kiptohanock.

Hobbling across the porch with the help of his cane, Mr.

Keller found them on the steps, gazing at the myriad of stars. He cleared his throat and grinned. "Congratulations."

She and Sawyer darted their eyes at each other and smiled.

"Got a proposition for you two. I'm too old to manage the farm and the horses. I haven't been able to get out of my head what you shared with me about your childhood, Sawyer."

Sawyer's brow furrowed.

Mr. Keller nodded. "The dream you shared with me… How you wished a place like my farm had existed for you and your sister. As a place for separated foster siblings to reunite for a week of summer camp."

Honey caught hold of Sawyer's hand.

Mr. Keller sighed. "Fact is, I've got more money than I'll ever spend. I've lived a self-absorbed life. Taking more than I've given. And it's time—long past time—for me to leave something beyond myself when I go to my reward."

Sawyer frowned. "I don't understand, sir. What is it you're proposing?"

Mr. Keller leaned both hands on the cane. "I'm proposing to build a set of cabins on the property. Fill out the necessary paperwork and get licensed with Social Services."

The old man rubbed his grizzled chin. "I haven't been sitting on my hands the whole time I was in rehab, son. I've done the math and already got the paperwork started with county agencies. I figure maybe by June we could be up and running. Offer equestrian and recreational boating activities to a different set of Accomack foster children each week of summer."

Sawyer squeezed Honey's fingers. "That sounds wonderful, Mr. Keller. For the children to be able to reunite at least for one week with their siblings…"

Mr. Keller pursed his mouth. "I'm also thinking we'll

need to hire staff, experts in their field. Counselors to deal with the deeper issues. Not only give them the best of the Eastern Shore, but provide life skills, too." He angled toward the party inside the house. "Never had kids of my own, you see."

"Keller's Kids Camp." Honey smiled. "You'll transform lives. A work of eternal significance."

Mr. Keller's eyes widened. "I hadn't given the whole idea a name." He shuffled his feet on the weathered planks of the porch.

"She's right." Sawyer swallowed. "A work of eternal significance in these throwaway kids lives."

Mr. Keller lifted his chin. "Ain't nobody gonna be a throwaway on my watch."

Honey tilted her head. "You said, 'we'll' make a difference. What do you mean, Mr. Keller?"

Mr. Keller angled toward Sawyer. "I know this woman of yours runs an inn, but I'd like you to consider becoming the director of this venture I'm proposing. I'd supply the startup money and property. You'd supply the brains and brawn for the day-to-day operation."

Sawyer gasped. "Me?"

"Of course, you." Mr. Keller shot a look at Honey. "We've got our work cut out for us, young lady, to bolster this lad's flagging self-confidence."

Sawyer swiveled toward her. "But Honey, summer is your busiest season."

"This is your dream. And because it's your dream, Sawyer Kole, it's my dream, too." She ran the pad of her thumb across his high cheekbone. "You gave me back my dream. Now it's your turn. We'll make it work, I promise you."

"What do you say, young feller?"

Sawyer gazed deep and long into her eyes. "Are you

sure?" he whispered. "It's too late for my sister and me, but if other kids could..." He blinked back the moisture.

Honey hugged his arm. "Horses. The sea. And foster kids. What could be better? Tell the man you'll do it."

Sawyer stuck out his hand. "If you're sure, Mr. Keller, I gladly accept. It'll cost a fortune to create and maintain..."

Mr. Keller grasped his hand. "You let me worry about that. Best use I'll ever make of all that money my grand-pappy earned."

They shook on it.

"It's a deal then." Mr. Keller moved toward the front door. "I'm going to whet my whistle, but I'll be in touch with further details."

He paused on the threshold, his head cocked. "But not until the honeymoon's over." He winked at them before disappearing into the house.

Sawyer pulled Honey into an embrace. "Honeymoon's never going to be over, is it, Mrs. Kole?" He grimaced at the overflowing lodge. "That is if we can ever get it officially started."

Honey laughed.

But a few hours later, she waved the last of the guests and her family goodbye. Their honeymoon night would be spent alone at the lodge before she and Sawyer drove to a quaint bed and breakfast on an isolated North Carolina barrier island via ferry. Market research, Honey had teased.

Sawyer arched his brow and let her know what he thought of her plan. With his lips.

A perfect night, she took one last look at the stars above the roofline of the porch. A perfect wedding. And the real adventure only just beginning.

The sound of an old-fashioned melody wafted from the interior of the house. Her breath hitching, Honey put her hand to the strand of pearls at her throat.

"Mrs. Kole."

She turned, the train of her dress swirling around her legs. Out of his uniform coat, Sawyer had rolled the sleeves of his shirt, exposing the strong, corded muscles of his forearms. Hands in his pockets, he propped against the frame of the door.

The music flowed from the Victrola, floating onto the porch.

Straightening, Sawyer held out his hand. Emotions rippled across his face. Joy. Such love. A fierce vulnerability. His gaze traveled to her mouth. And lingered.

Her heart beating faster than the 3/4 time of the waltz, she took his hand. Her eyes locked onto his. And his eyes went opaque, a smoky blue.

With her hand clasped in his and his other arm around her waist, she placed her free hand on the broad length of his shoulder.

Elbow up and carriage erect, he never took his eyes off her face. His hold never wavered as he led Honey in the waltz.

"Let me call you, sweetheart..." he crooned in that lovely baritone of his. "I'm in love with you..." Something flickered in his eyes. "Let me hear you whisper that you love me, too..."

The music and the words flowed over her like gentle rain.

"Keep the love light glowing in your eyes so true—"

Her heart skipped a beat.

He cradled her face between his hands. And she watched his love for her glow in his eyes so blue.

"Let me call you sweetheart..." His voice thickened.

Tears burned at the back of Honey's eyelids. A lifetime of joy with this man awaited. Who knew a cowboy Coastie could be so achingly romantic?

"I'm in love..." she whispered. "With...you..."

The melody flowed around them, weaving a spell of love's possibilities.

* * * * *

Dear Reader,

Thanks for traveling with me to the fictional seaside village of Kiptohanock. The Eastern Shore of Virginia is a real and very dear place to me. I visited the Eastern Shore for the first time at the age of twenty-one. The summer I lived there getting to know the wonderful people and unique culture of the Shore was transformational. And after all these years, I revisit this splendid Tidewater destination as often as I can with my family.

Honey and Sawyer grapple with doubt, anger and faith throughout this story. If we live long enough, most of us will experience the pain of loss. But though life is often hard, God is always good. And enough for our every need—past, present or future. My prayer, dear reader, is that when difficulties come, we would run *to* Him and not away. That though we might never understand the why, we'd be willing to take that enormous step of faith to believe He is for us. His love for us is summed up by two remarkable truths: grace—getting what we don't deserve, and mercy—not getting what we do deserve. Because, praise God, this world isn't our final home.

I love the Eastern Shore and its people. I hope you have enjoyed taking this journey of faith with me, Honey and Sawyer. I would also love to hear from you. You may email me at lisa@lisacarterauthor.com or visit www.lisacarterauthor.com.

And if you can, hug a Coastie today.

Wishing you fair winds and following seas,
Lisa Carter

When a young woman is being stalked, can she count on her handsome bodyguard to protect her?

Read on for a sneak preview of
HER RANCHER BODYGUARD,
the next book in the series
MARTIN'S CROSSING.

When Kayla had discovered she had a bodyguard, she hadn't expected this. He should be in the background, quietly observing. Her father was a lawyer and a politician; she'd seen bodyguards and knew how they did their jobs. And yet here she sat with this family, her bodyguard talking of cattle and fixing fence as his sisters tried to cajole him into taking them to look at a pair of horses owned by Kayla's brother.

A hand settled on her back. She glanced at the man next to her, his dark eyes crinkled at the corners and his mouth quirked, revealing a dimple in his left cheek.

Boone opened his mouth as if to say something but a heavy knock on the front door interrupted. He pushed away from the table and gave them all an apologetic look.

"I think I'll get that." His gaze landed on Kayla. "You stay right where you are until I say otherwise."

"They wouldn't come here," she said. And she'd meant to sound strong; instead it came out like a question.

"We don't know what they would or wouldn't do, because we don't know who they are. Stay." Boone walked away, his brother Jase getting up and going after him.

Kayla avoided looking at his family, who still remained at the table. Conversation had of course ended. She knew they were looking at her. She knew that she had invaded their life.

And she knew that her bodyguard might seem like a relaxed cowboy, but he wasn't. He was the man standing between her and the unknown.

LIEXP0516

"Make another move, and I'll shoot you where you stand..." He trailed off, jaw sagging. Had he entered the wrong house?

"Don't shoot! I can explain! I—I have a letter. From Will Canfield." A petite dark-haired woman standing on the other side of his table lifted an envelope in silent entreaty.

At the mention of his friend's name, he slowly lowered his weapon. But his defensive instincts still surged through him. When he didn't speak, she gestured limply to the ornate leather trunks stacked on either side of his bedroom door. "Mr. Canfield was supposed to meet us at the station. His porter arrived in his stead... Simon was his name. He said something about a posse and outlaws." A delicate shudder shook her frame. "He said you wouldn't mind if we brought these inside. I do apologize for invading your home like this, but I had no idea when you would return, and it is June out there."

Her gaze roamed his face, her light brown eyes widening ever so slightly as they encountered his scars. It was like this every time. He braced himself for the inevitable disgust. Pity. Revulsion. Told himself again it didn't matter.

When her expression reflected nothing more than curiosity, irrational anger flooded him.

"What are you doing in my home?" he snapped. "How do you know Will?"

"I'm Constance Miller. I'm the bride Mr. Canfield sent for."

"Will's already got a wife."

Pink kissed her cheekbones. "Not for him. For you."

His throat closed. He wouldn't have.

"I was summoned to Cowboy Creek to be your bride. Your friend didn't tell you." A sharp crease brought her brows together.

"I'm afraid not." Slipping off his worn Stetson, Noah hooked it on the chair and dipped his head toward the crumpled parchment. "May I?"

Miss Miller didn't appear inclined to approach him, so he laid his gun on the mantel and crossed to the square table. He took the envelope she extended across to him and slipped the letter free. The handwriting was unmistakable. Heat climbed up his neck as he read the description of himself. He stuffed it back inside and tossed it onto the tabletop. "I'm afraid you've come all the way out here for nothing. The trip was a waste, Miss Miller. I am not, nor will I ever be, in the market for a bride."